不朽的失眠。

Immortal Sleeplessness

張曉風 散文　中英對照

欣賞中文與英文雙美

中譯英本非易事，除了了解字面意義外，還要懂得作者筆下的意境。中華民國筆會多年來秉持「團結優秀作家，提高創作水準，譯介本國當代作品，促進國際文化交流」之宗旨，在歷任主編殷張蘭熙、齊邦媛、宋美王華、彭鏡禧、張惠娟、高天恩、梁欣榮等教授主事下，精選優秀的中文作品，翻成英文，推廣至全球各地愛好中文之美的人士。多年來，政府致力推廣優質國內文學作品，希冀藉由台灣優秀的文化競爭力，以期與國際接軌，因此九歌出版社與中華民國筆會合作，精選好看好讀的名家文章，並配合精確的英文翻譯，讓國人同時領略中英雙種語言之美，與政府拓展國人國際觀的理念目標，相輔相成。

本系列以名家作品為主，首先推出多位知名散文家的散文，計有張曉風、廖玉蕙、席慕蓉等。本書為名散文家張曉風的作品中英對照《不朽的失眠：張曉風散文中英對照》。曉風老師的散文具備高度的精密性與藝術性；她寫宇宙萬物的大道理，也寫多彩繽紛的日常生活，更關照社會民生；不論描人繪景，或是敘事抒情，文字皆洗鍊生動，用句遣詞剛柔並濟，讀者在潛移默化間得著撫慰與激勵。

內容上，精選曉風老師名作：有替懷才不遇的詩人張繼訴說不得志心情的〈不朽的失眠〉，有省思身分證明的〈我撿到一張身分證〉，有訴說香江景致的〈不是遊記〉，更有青春情懷的〈你真好，你就像我少年伊辰〉等共11篇散文。而編排上則採用中文與英文對照編排方式，讓愛好中文散文者，閱讀名家作品，豐富自己的用字遣詞，增進寫作能力。學習中文人士可藉由精采的散文作品中英對照，了解道地優雅的中文；閱讀英文及翻譯研究者，忠實領略到文學之美。期待這一套書為中西方文學打開交流與了解之門。

編者

目　錄

003　欣賞中文與英文雙美

007　不朽的失眠　Immortal Sleeplessness
　　　杜南馨／譯

021　就讓他們不知道吧！　Just Let Them Not Know!
　　　陳懿貞／譯

067　你真好，你就像我少年伊辰　You're So Good, You're Just Like Me When I Was Young
　　　彭安之／譯

077　1230點　1,230 Spots
　　　彭鏡禧／譯

127　我撿到了一張身分證　Finding An ID
　　　康士林／譯

149　月，闕也　The Moon, The Imperfect
　　　胡守芳／譯

163　十月的陽光 October Sun
　　施鐵民／譯

183　不是遊記 Not a Travelogue
　　吳敏嘉／譯

219　畫　晴 Painting a Sunny Day
　　吳敏嘉／譯

243　我不知道怎樣回答 I Don't Know How to Answer
　　吳敏嘉／譯

255　給我一個解釋 Give Me an Explanation
　　吳敏嘉／譯

不朽的失眠

Immortal Sleeplessness

杜南馨／譯

Translated by Nancy Du

　　既然無眠，他推枕而起，摸黑寫下「楓橋夜泊」四字。然後，就把其餘二十八個字照抄下來。我說「照抄」，是因為那二十八個字在他心底已像白牆上的黑字一樣分明凸顯：

　　　　月落烏啼霜滿天　　江楓漁火對愁眠

　　　　姑蘇城外寒山寺　　夜半鐘聲到客船

他落榜了！一千二百年前。
榜紙那麼大那麼長，

然而，就是沒有他的名字。啊！竟單單容不下他的名字「張繼」那兩個字。

考中的人，姓名一筆一劃寫在榜單上，天下皆知。奇怪的是，在他的感覺裡，考不上才更是天下皆知，這件事，令他羞慚沮喪。

離開京城吧！議好了價，他踏上小舟。本來預期的情節不是這樣的，本來也許有個插花遊街、馬蹄輕疾的風流，有衣錦還鄉袍笏加身的榮耀。然而，寒窗十年，雖有他的懸樑刺股，瓊林宴上，卻並沒有他的一角席次。

船行似風。

He didn't make it ! One thousand two hundred years ago. On that big and lengthy scroll of names, only his was missing. Why, could it not just hold the two simple characters of his name, Chang Chi?

The ones that made it, their names were written stroke for stroke on the public bulletin board. An announcement to the world. Strangely, he felt, his failure was even more of an announcement to the world. This shamed and depressed him.

Leave the imperial city! Once a price was fixed, he boarded a small boat. This was not the way the story was supposed to evolve, originally perhaps he would be adorned with flowers and he would parade in the streets, ever so debonair while his horse trotted gently in the wind. He would be filled with the glory of returning home decorated and honored. But despite his ten years of careful study and its share of struggle and pain[1], there was no seat for him at the Chung Lin Feast[2].

The boat sailed as fast as the wind.

1.———*In Chinese, this literally means to tie one's hair on a house beam and jab at oneself with an awl to keep oneself awake. It refers to the extreme hardships some examinees experienced in order to prepare for their official examinations.*

2.———*The Chung Lin Feast was a feast hosted by the emperor in honor of the successful examinees of the imperial examination.*

　　江楓如火，在岸上舉著冷冷的燼焰，這天黃昏，船，來到了蘇州。但，這美麗的古城，對張繼而言，也無非是另一個觸動愁情的地方。

　　如果說白天有什麼該做的事，對一個讀書人而言，就是讀書吧！夜晚呢？夜晚該睡覺以便養足精神第二天再讀。然而，今夜是一個憂傷的夜晚，在異鄉，在江畔，在秋冷雁高的季節，容許一個落魄的士子放肆他的憂傷。江水，可以無限度的收納古往今來一切不順遂之人的淚水。

　　這樣的夜晚，殘酷的坐著，親自聽自己的心正被什麼東西囓食而一分一分消失的聲音。並且眼睜睜地看著自己的生命如勁風中的殘燈，所有的力氣都花在抗拒，油快盡了，微火每一剎那都可能熄滅。然而，可恨的是，終其一生，它都不曾華美燦爛過啊！

The maples by the river bank appear as if on fire, its cold flames lifted high. That day at dusk, the boat docked at Suchou. But to Chang Chi, this beautiful ancient city was just another place that touched his sorrow.

To a scholar, if there was one thing he had to do during the day, it was to study. And at night? Nights were for sleeping so you had enough stamina to continue studying the following day. But, tonight was a melancholic evening. Tonight, in a faraway land, by the river bank, during the cold season of autumn where wild geese flew overhead, a down and out scholar was permitted to give full vent to his sorrow. The river, throughout the years, had the capacity to swallow infinitely the tears of the unblessed.

A night like this, he sat without any sympathy for himself, listening to the sound of his own heart disintegrating bit by bit as something gnawed at it. He look wide-eyed at his own life dwindling like an old lamp in a strong wind, with every ounce of energy spent resisting. The oil was almost out, the weak flame would die any moment. But the hateful truth was, throughout his life, the flame had never once shone brightly and resplendently!

江水睡了，船睡了，船家睡了，岸上的人也睡了。唯有他，張繼，醒著，夜愈深，愈清醒，清醒如敗葉落餘的枯樹，似樑燕飛去的空巢。

起先，是睡眠排拒了他（也罷，這半生，不是處處都遭排拒嗎？）而後，是他在賭氣，好，無眠就無眠，長夜獨醒，就乾脆徹底來為自己驗傷，有何不可？

月亮西斜了，一副意興闌珊的樣子。有烏啼，粗嘎嘶啞，是烏鴉。那月亮被牠一聲聲叫得更黯淡了。江岸上，想已霜結千草。夜空裡，星子亦如清霜，一粒粒冷絕悽絕。

江上漁火二三，他們在幹什麼？在捕魚吧？或者，蝦？他們也會有撒空網的時候嗎？世路艱辛啊！

The river slept. The boat slept. The boatman slept. The people on the shore also slept. Only he, Chang Chi, was awake. The deeper night fell, the more awake he became. Awake as a dying tree with very few leaves hanging; awake as an empty swallow's nest deserted on the roof beam.

At first, sleep refused him (but then, most of his life, wasn't he constantly being refused wherever he went?) Then in anger, his resolve strengthened. Fine, sleepless he would remain. Being the only one awake in the long night, he would give his scars a thorough examination. What was there to prevent him?

The moon slanted westward, appearing dispirited. A bird cawed hoarsely. It was a crow. Cowering under the cries of the crow, the moon looked even more crestfallen. He imagined frost forming on the vast spread of grass on the bank. In the night sky, the stars looked also like clear frost, each crystal cold and cutting to the core.

There was a sparse scattering of light from the fishing boats on the river. What were they doing? Catching fish? Or shrimp?

即使瀟灑的捕魚人，也不免投身在風波裡吧？

然而，能辛苦工作，也是一項幸福呢！今夜，月自光其光，霜自冷其冷，安心的人在安眠，工作的人去工作。只有我張繼，是天不管地不收的一個，是既沒有權利去工作，也沒福氣去睡眠的一個……。

鐘聲響了，這奇怪的深夜的寒山寺鐘聲。一般寺廟，都是暮鼓晨鐘，寒山寺卻敲「夜半鐘」，用以警世。鐘聲貼著水面傳來，在別人，那聲音只是睡夢中模糊的襯底音樂。在他，卻一記一記都撞擊在心坎上，正中要害。鐘聲那麼美麗，但鐘自己到底是痛還不是不痛呢？

既然無眠，他推枕而起，摸黑寫下「楓橋夜泊」

Do they ever cast out nets that return without any catch? Life was hard. Even the carefree fishermen must sometimes get tangled in the wind and waves, surely?

But to be able to work hard was also a blessing. Tonight, the moon shone as moons do, the frost was cold as frost is generally, the sleeping were asleep, the working were at work. There was only he left. Chang Chi, a preson who was discarded by heaven and jilted by earth. One who did not have the right to work, nor the fortune to sleep...

A bell rang, late at night, eerily, from the Cold Mountain Temple. Generally, temples tolled bells in the morning and beat drums in the evening. But the Cold Mountain Temple rang its bell in the middle of the night as a warning to the masses. The sound of the bell rode on the water and travelled over. To others, the sound was just a vague sort of background music in their dreams. To him, the sound banged hard against his heart, right to his very hurt. The bell sounded hauntingly beautiful, but did the bell itself feel pain?

As sleep eluded him, he pushed aside his pillow and rose. In

四字。然後，就把其餘二十八個字照抄下來。我說
「照抄」，是因為那二十八個字在他心底已像白牆上
的黑字一樣分明凸顯：

> 月落烏啼霜滿天
> 江楓漁火對愁眠
> 姑蘇城外寒山寺
> 夜半鐘聲到客船

感謝上蒼，如果沒有落第的張繼，詩的歷史上便
少了一首好詩，我們的某一種心情，就沒有人來為我
們一語道破。

一千二百年過去了，那張長長的榜單上（就是張
繼擠不進去那張金榜）曾經出現過的狀元是誰？哈！
誰管他是誰？真正被記得的名字是「落第者張繼」。

the dark, he wrote down the words 'Mooring at Night by Maple Bridge.' Then, he copied the other twenty-eight characters down one by one. I say copied because the other twenty-eight characters were as clear as black ink on the white wall of his consciousness:

Moon setting, crow cawing, frost filling the sky.
Through river maples, fisherman flares confronting troubled sleep.
Outside Kusu Cith, Cold Mountain Temple—
Late at night the sound of its bell reaches a traveler's boat.[3]

Thank god. Were it not for Chang Chi who failed his examination, a great poem would be missing from the history of poetry. There would be no one to hit a certain mood of ours right in the eye.

One thousand two hundred years have since passed. Who was the top examinee on that long public notice (that golden scroll that Chang Chi could not squeeze into)? Ha, who cares? The name that we really remember is Chang Chi, the one that failed.

3.———*Adapted from the Columbia Book of Chinese Poetry-from Early Times to the Thirteenth Century, translated and edited by Burton Watson, N. Y. Columbia University Press, 1984. Watson's title of the poem: "Tying up for the Night at Maple River Bridge'.*

有人會記得那一年的狀元披紅遊街的盛況嗎？不！我們只記得秋夜的客船上那個失意的人，以及他那場不朽的失眠。

——原載一九九五年七月十日《中國時報》

收入九歌版《這杯咖啡的溫度剛好》（1996年）

Does any one recall the top scoring scholar of that year and the festive occasion of his parade in the streets? No, we only remember that autumn evening with the disillusioned man on the small boat. And his immortal sleeplessness.

"The Chinese PEN" **Autumn, 1995**

就讓他們不知道吧！

Just Let Them Not Know!

陳懿貞／譯　施堂模／審訂

Translated by Chen I-djen　Revised by Tom Sellari

　　讓我知道吧！說給我聽那悽慘的情由！讓我知道更多！我已是成年人，有夠強的心肌，可以聽最傷心的故事，有夠硬的肩膀，可以挑起如山的憂患，有夠鹹的眼淚，可以為淚枯的人致哀。

當三月破二月而來

謹以此文贈給

在此番春郊上

千里馳走的青年

我一個人到機場接丈夫，他從泰國難民營回來。

「這是我給你買的。」坐上車，他迫不及待的從破帆布包裡拿出一個小紙包：「這是苗人的銀器，舊舊黯黯的，好便宜，我一看就知道你會喜歡……」

從大一算起，認識他有二十二年了，他的語調一向又急又快：「苗人的手工很特別，難民裡好多是苗人，真可憐，前不久，他們集體抗暴，結果共產黨打

I went alone to the airport to meet my husband, who was returning from visiting refugee camps in Thailand.

"I bought this for you." As soon as we had gotten into the car he took out a small package from his old canvas bag. "It's a silver piece made by the Miao people, somewhat tarnished, very inexpensive. The moment I saw it, I knew you would like it."

I have known him for twenty-two years, ever since my freshman year of college. He always talked a blue streak. "The handicrafts of the Miao people are quite unique. There are a lot of Miao among the refugees. They are really pitiful. Not too long ago, they

不過他們，就施放毒氣，一下死了幾萬人，倒得滿山遍野……」

沉黯的舊銀器一下在手裡冷了下來。小學課本上背過「漢、滿、蒙、回、藏、苗」，一直就單純的相信——「苗子」是同胞，雖然並沒有看過一個「苗子」，但書總是錯不了的。正好像歌裡面唱的「山川壯麗，物產豐隆」是錯不了的一樣。

而何竟在高速公路急馳的冷氣車裡，我第一次手觸一件苗人的銀器，竟伴隨著這樣一個悲慘的故事？

「有個女孩，從越南來，是華僑，二十幾歲吧！」他說：「她一直就在逃難，從會走大概就在

collectively rebelled against tyranny. When the communists could not subdue them they used poison gas. Tens of thousands died, all over the mountainside and in the fields..."

Suddenly this tarnished piece of old silver felt very cold in my hands. In my elementary school days I learned the names of the six peoples of our country, the Han, the Manchus, the Mongolians, the Muhammedan, the Tibetans, and the Miao, and I had always simply believed that the Miao were one of us. I had never met a Miao, but surely the books could not be wrong. I believed in them implicitly just as I believed in the songs which described our country with such words as "majestic mountains, beautiful rivers, overabundance of natural resources."[1] The songs could not be wrong.

Why did it have to be just as we were speeding along the super highway in an air-conditioned car that my hands came into contact for the first time with a piece of Miao silverwork which had brought with it such a heat-breaking story?

"There was a girl from Vietnam. She was an overseas Chinese, about twenty." He began to tell me the story. "She had been on

---

1.———lines from the National Flag Song（國旗歌）.

逃，逃了十幾年了，她這輩子唯一的『經歷』就是逃難，我故意問她：『你們為什麼要逃呢？大不了一死，逃難這麼慘，何必逃呢？』她笑起來，『死？共產黨那有這麼好，肯讓你死，死當然不可怕，但他們關你、餓你、打你、侮辱你、讓你每分鐘恐懼，覺得求死無門，我們從前做苦工，每天找不到一定份量的糞做肥料就不准吃飯，而且，女孩子還拉去強姦……你從台灣來的吧？哈，台灣來的人最不知道什麼是共產黨了！』」

「還有個女孩子，」丈夫接著說：「在難民營裡居然碰到了散開的家人……」

「這一下可團圓了！」我終於插進嘴。

the run for over ten years, probably ever since she'd learned to walk. Her only experience in life was that of a refugee on the run. I asked her a loaded question, 'Why do you people keep running? The worst that could happen would be death, and to be forever on the run is a miserable way to live. Why do you keep running?' She laughed and said, 'Death? Do you think that the communists would be so good as to let us die? Death in itself is not to be feared, but they lock you up, starve you, beat you, humiliate you, and they instill so much fear in you every minute of the day that you wish you were dead. At one time we were engaged in hard labor. If we failed to collect our daily quota of manure which was to be used as fertilizer, we would not be allowed to eat, and the girls would be subject to rape... You must be from Taiwan. People from Taiwan know the least about the communists...'"

"There was this other girl," he continued, "She actually chanced upon her lost family in the refugee camp..."

"Then they were able to have a happy reunion." I finally got a word in.

「不，他們分了手，一半去了加拿大，一半去了法國——他們說，亂世裡，一家人千萬不要走在一起，弄不好一起死光，香火就斷了，寧可分開，只要有一個人活著，這個家就沒有斷……」

我急速地別過頭去，夏日午後明豔的軟枝黃蟬在路側嘩然飛騰，像萬千迅速的流矢。

回到家裡，小男孩和小女孩正在冰箱裡找可可冰出來吃，看見爸爸回來一起來討玩具。

「別胡鬧，難民營裡那有玩具賣！」

「難民營裡也有小孩子呀！」小女孩理直氣壯。

"No, they went their separate ways. Half of them went to Canada, half to France. They said that in these troubled times a family mustn't stay together, for if something should happen they would all perish, and the family line would end there. Better to separate a family; as long as one member is alive, the family lives on..."

I hastily turned my head aside. In the summer afternoon the colorful yellow of the flowering vines clambering over the sloping embankment along the side of the road flew past us like thousands of speeding arrows.

When we got home our little boy and little girl were searching in the refrigerator for cocoa ice. As soon as they saw their daddy they asked him for toys.

"Don't be ridiculous. How can there be toys for sale in refugee camps?"

"There are children in refugee camps too." The little girl was very righteous about it.

　　「怪不得那個女孩子說，全世界最不知道共產黨
是什麼的，就是台灣！」丈夫嘆了一口氣。

　　我轉過頭去，只見兄妹倆正合力用勺子挖可可
冰，吃得像平劇裡的三花臉。我要讓他們知道西南山
區裡成萬的苗子屍骨在森林裡腐化生蛆嗎？我要讓他
們知道逃難隊裡無助的母親終於同意大家的意見掐死
孩子，以免他啼哭不止而殃及眾人嗎？今夜臨睡前，
我忍心講那個一陣毒氣數萬屍體蓋滿青山的故事嗎？

　　「就讓他們不知道吧！」我幽幽的說。

　　　　　　　　　　　　∽

　　曾有一夜，在芝加哥，唐人街，穿過黃魚和青蟹

"No wonder that girl said that in all world, the people in Taiwan know the least about communists." My husband heaved a big sigh.

I turned around and saw that the children were engaged in a joint venture of digging into the cocoa ice with spoons, smearing their faces until they looked like the painted faces in Chinese operas. Did I want to let them know that in the forests in the southwestern mountain region tens of thousands of dead bodies of the Miao people were rotting away and covered with maggots? Did I want to let them know that in one group of refugees a hapless mother finally had to submit helplessly to public demand and strangle her child so that his ceaseless crying would not bring retribution upon them all? Tonight at bedtime would I have the heart to repeat the story about green mountains covered with tens of thousands of dead bodies killed by poison gas?

"Just let them not know about it!" I said mournfully to myself.

⅌

One night, in a big hall in Chicago, in Chinatown, we were

的氣味，穿過黃梅調和「十面埋伏」的琵琶曲，我們在一所大堂裡演唱。會後，一個精乾瘦小的中年人，走來握手。

「三十年了，我在大陸上參加過多少晚會，全是火藥氣味的，你們的不同，你們的一聽就知道有愛。」

兒子剛好走過，我拉著他說：
「來叫『朱伯伯』。」

兒子順從的叫了，故國萬里，一別三十年，浩浩的人海煙波上，今夕停舟暫相問。不問是否同鄉，只問是否「同族」吧，一聲朱伯伯，也是一番相存相恤之心，我對兒子說：「朱伯伯從北平來，今天是第一天到芝加哥。」兒子的眼睛忽然睜得銅鈴大，我一笑揮手，打發他去端一杯茶。人生百年，那裡不是驛站？三十年的憂患，半生的委屈，一筆一劃像史書一樣精確的寫在他的臉上，我要唸給孩子聽嗎？不要，

presenting a show, over the smell of haddock and crabs, and over the sounds of *Hwang Mei* melodies and the music of *Pi Pa* lutes. Afterwards, a dried-up little middle-aged man came over and shook my hand.

"It has been thirty years since I attended many such evening events on the mainland. They all had the smell of gun powder. Yours is different. Just listening to you I know there is love."

Just then my son walked by. I stopped him and told him, "Say hello to 'Uncle Chu.'"

He did. Our homeland lies ten thousand *li* away, and it has been thirty years since we left. Life is like a vast misty sea, and that night two boats stopped for a while to exchange greetings. It did not matter if we came from the same province, it only mattered that we were of the same *people*. Addressing him as "Uncle Chu" was only an expression of kinship and compassion. I told my son, "Uncle Chu just came from Peiping. This is his first day in Chicago." My son opened his eyes wide as bells. I smiled and waved him away to get us a cup of tea. In a lifetime's journey of one hundred years every stop is a way station. Thirty years of

只一聲朱伯伯，便明日天涯了，至於那三十年的浩劫就讓孩子不甚知道吧！

8

出紐約城郊，許忽然指著一條路說：

「這附近，住了我一個朋友，他前兩年把他母親接出來，沒想到那老母親出來以後天天讚美歌頌毛澤東，朋友覺得奇怪，怎麼人到了美國還如此？反駁幾次，不見效，也只好隨她嘮嘮叨叨去說了。更奇怪的是事隔半年，她老人家忽然又破口大罵毛澤東，連最難聽的話都罵出來了，朋友簡直被她嚇呆了，她老人家卻說：『我剛來的時候當然不敢罵啦，我怎麼知道你們跟他們不是一條線的？我試了半年，才知道你們不是，現在我敢罵了！』」

worries, half a lifetime of suffering, were clearly etched on his face, stroke by stroke, telling a story as true as the records of any history books. Did I want to read it to my children? No. Just call him Uncle Chu and let it go at that; tomorrow will find us at far ends of the world. As for those disastrous thirty years, let's just not let the children know too much about them!

ॐ

One day as we were leaving the outskirts of New York City my friend Hsu suddenly said to me, pointing to a road off the highway, "A friend of mine lives around here. He brought his mother out of China two years ago. To his surprise, the old lady sang the praises of Mao Tze-tung day in and day out. My friend was curious. Why was she keeping it up even in America? They argued a number of times, all to no avail. He had no choice but to leave her be. What was even stranger was that half a year later all of a sudden she started to curse Mao Tze-tung using the most awful language. My friend was stunned. She then explained, 'When I first came I of course did not dare to curse him. How was I to know if you were on his side or not? I tested you for half a year. Now I know you are not, so I now dare to curse him.'"

五千年孝慈傳家的國度，落得母親不敢相信兒子，這樣的事說給誰聽呢？盈月一般光潤的年輕耳朵只慣於聽吉他的磁磁柔柔的聲音，這樣的故事說給誰聽呢？華爾街的股票沉沉落落，藍儂的金唱片銷了幾百幾十萬了？福特夫人拉面皮的手術很成功吧？福特總統自己在越南淪亡之日在美國機場上抱起一個空運來的小難民，照片效果拍得極好⋯⋯誰有興趣聽一個長達十億幕的大型悲劇？不要知道吧，就讓他們不知道吧！

&

許後來自己也回了大陸一趟，一出廣州，就在香港大病一場。

「怎麼能不病？」他說：「一個月，我每天旅行，每到一個地方，見到老朋友談起三十年來受的痛

Here was a story of a mother who dared not trust her own son, and it concerned two people from a country which prided itself on five thousand years of filial traditions. To whom could I tell such a story? The young ears of today have only been exposed to the soft music of guitars. To whom could I tell such a story? On Wall Street the stocks plunge. How many millions of Lennon's gold records have been sold? Was Mrs. Ford's face-lift a success? On the day Vietnam fell, there was a picture of President Ford at an airport holding a young refugee who had been air-lifted over. The picture was very effective...Who would be interested in listening to a colossal tragedy that would continue on and on for one billion acts? They don't want to know, so just let them not know!

ॐ

My friend Hsu later went back to China. On his way out of the country, as soon as he left Canton and reached Hong Kong, he became ill.

"How can anybody not become ill?" he said. "I have been travelling for a month. Wherever I went, whenever I met with old

苦冤屈就大哭一場，連著一個月天天慟哭，怎麼能不
病？」

　　他後來又遇見一位在困境中曾受他接濟過的朋
友，那朋友窮得身無長物，卻又拚命想找出一件東西
來相酬，最後他翻出一枚刻著自己名字的舊圖章，趑
趑趄趄萬分惶愧的遞給許，並且說：「石頭是好石
頭，你把我的名字磨掉就是了，你還可以用的，我反
正用不著。」

　　許不忍拿，又不忍不拿，唯恐傷到朋友的自尊。

　　「我怎麼可以磨掉我朋友的名字呢？」坐在西寧
南路喧譁的海鮮店裡，許悲傷的說。

　　他朋友的名字和他的一生其實早就磨掉了，十億
人口的生命和尊嚴早就磨掉了，又豈在這一方小小的

friends we talked about their sufferings and grievances of the last thirty years, and we cried. How can anyone not be ill from crying for a full month?"

Hsu later came across a friend whom he had helped in his moments of need. The friend was very poor, and he had no personal belongings of any kind, yet he wanted desperately to give my friend something as a token of his gratitude. Finally he found on old personal seal of his and handed it over to Hsu, with embarrassed hesitancy, saying, "The stone is a good one. Rub my name off, and you can use it again. In any event I have no use for it."

Hsu could not bring himself to accept it, yet a refusal would certainly hurt his friend's feelings.

"How can I ever rub my friend's name off?" In a seafood restaurant on His-ning South Road, Hsu asked this question with great sadness in his voice.

Actually the name and the life of his friend had been rubbed off long ago. The lives and dignity of a billion people have all been

玉石。

但，這樣的事，去告訴誰呢？就讓世人不知道
吧！

∞

其實，不幸的豈只是那塊焦土上的人？連我們，
活在這常翠島上的人不也常是悲傷的嗎？讀大學的
時候常到一位老教授家去，所謂家，只是山間的半邊
小屋，臥房客廳飯廳和書房全在一起，牆上是一幀師
母的照片，手繪的彩色，沉豔淒涼，安靜地俯視著教
授。照片裡的人像被魔法定住了，歲歲年年，永遠微
微驚愕地睜著一雙溫柔的眼睛，粗黑的麻花大辮垂向
胸前。

「唉，想不開啊，」教授嘆氣：「我叫她出來，
叫她出來，她說等穀子賣了就走，穀子往下跌，她捨

erased, so what could this little piece of jade matter?

But to whom could I tell a story like this? Just let the world not know about it!

℞

The fact was that the people on that scorched land were not the only unlucky ones. Haven't we who live on this evergreen island also had our share of grief? When I was in college I often visited an old professor. His so-called home was no more than half a room leaning against the side of a hill, and it served as his bedroom, living room, dining room, and study. On the wall was a hand-painted photograph of his beautiful wife gazing sadly down at him in deep melancholy. It was as if she were frozen in time by the hand of magic, and year after year her gentle eyes always held a slightly startled look, and her thick black braid was always hanging down over her shoulder, lying against her breast.

"Well, she couldn't let go," said the professor with a sigh. "I told her to leave; I told her to. She said she would as soon as she

不得啊，自家田裡收的穀子啊！她寫信說，等穀價稍微漲一點，稍微漲一點點，她賣了就走，晚了，走不成了，就這樣⋯⋯」

闔上《易經》，人生的窮通，人世的劫數又怎麼計算呢？

「人家說，女人的頭髮有布頭髮和絲頭髮，你師母是絲頭髮⋯⋯」

絲頭髮從牆上俯下，如何攀援呢？短短的山牆是千仞絕壁啊，這樣的故事，說給誰聽呢？像那半間老山屋，幽幽的，有一股綠霉的氣味，誰要聽呢？不要說吧，就讓不知道的人不知道吧！

sold the harvest of grain. The price of grain was falling, and she could not bring herself to sell. It was the harvest from our own land. She wrote that as soon as the price went back up, even a little, she would sell and leave. Then it was too late; she could not leave. Now..."

Close the *Book of Changes*. How can one figure out the success and failure of a life time? How can one predict the impending calamities of the world?

"It is said that women's hair can be classified into two types, the cottony type and the silky type. Your teacher's wife's is the silky type..."

She of the silky hair looked down from the wall. How can one climb up to reach her? The low wall, which was on the side of a hill, was a sheer precipice. To whom can I tell this story? Who would want to hear the story of half of an old room leaning against the side of a hill, dark and damp and smelling of mildew? Let's not talk about it. Let the people who do not know about it remain unknowing.

ॐ

「那一年，我們逃到鎮江，到了金山寺，」朋友黃以功說：「我和弟弟一起病了，弟弟死了，媽媽抱著我，等著，不知道我會不會死？」

我聽了，只覺詫異，金山寺，不是《白蛇傳》的金山寺嗎？金山寺應該是鐘鼓儼然金碧輝煌，昂昂然的坐落在山川形勝的地方才是啊！然後，鏗然一聲，法相莊嚴的法海和尚就披著金紅的袈裟走了出來，當頭一缽罩下，一切妖魔鬼怪無所逃……

但那一年的金山寺，一個蓬頭苦臉的婦人，在逃難的路上，腳下守著一個孩子的屍體，手中抱著垂死的另一個，此時此際，善於收妖的法海又能說什麼？

∽

"That year when we escaped to the city of Chengchiang and reached the Gold Mountain Temple," my friend Hwang Yi-kung told us, "both my brother and I became ill. My brother died. My mother held me against her bosom, waiting, not knowing whether or not I too would die."

I was very surprised to hear the story. Wasn't the Gold Mountain Temple the one in the opera *White Snake*? The Temple should be sitting majestically at a grand scenic spot, glittering in gold and resounding with the beat of drums and bells. And then, at the beat of a drum the monk Fa-hai in his red and gold buddhist robe would walk out in all his priestly dignity. And when he waved his magic urn all the demons and goblins would be trapped, and there would be no escape for any of them...

But in that particular year at the Gold Mountain Temple there was a women refugee on the run, her hair tangled and dishevelled, her face sad. At her feet lay the body of a dead child and in her arms that of one near death. At such a time and place, what would the

這樣的故事，我要說它嗎？就讓它湮沒無聞隨風而逝吧，就讓他們不知道吧！

&

沉冬、深夜，家人都睡了，我獨坐孤燈下，為姜成濤寫一首歌詞，他性急，有時竟半夜從巴黎打電話來催。

一個人兀坐著，題目已寫好：

「賣饅頭的老王，他接到了一封信。」

不是無話可寫，而是一時心如狂濤，不知怎樣收攏，不知怎樣把自己規規矩矩合韻合轍的收回一行行的格子裡去。我其實並不認得一個賣饅頭的老王，可是又覺得認識那人已經幾十年了，他常騎一輛破腳踏

Monk Fa-hai, known for his ability to subdue demons and goblins, say?

Did I want to tell this story? No. Let it be blown away quietly with the wind without leaving any trace. Let the people not know about it.

℘

One winter, in the deep of the night, I was sitting under a lone light to write a lyric for my friend Chiang Cheng-tao in Paris. He was an impetuous and impatient msn. He was likely to call from Paris in the middle of the night to hurry me.

I sat up straight in my chair. I had already thought of a topic: Lao Wang, the steamcd-bread vendor, receives a letter.

It wasn't that I had nothing to say. On the contrary, wild waves of thoughts were surfacing, and I did not know how to control them. I did not know how to put them down on paper, line after line according to the prescribed rules of rhyme and rhythm. I did not know a bread vendor called Lao Wang, yet I felt as if I had

車，嘎著和車子同音色的喉嚨吆喝著：

「包子——饅頭——豆沙包——」

　　他們差不多一例是北方人，黑臉膛，堅毅，卻不怎麼快樂的眼睛。他們賣白饅頭，也為大眾口味賣甜饅頭。黃昏，穿巷子，暮色裡背影像黑紙剪貼，在每一個大城小鎮……

　　而設若，有一天，他正在揉麵，忽然，一位鄉親輾轉帶一封髒爛泛黃的信來，信打開，殘酷而簡單，母親死了，在一九七〇……

　　我不認識老王，可是我知道那事是真的，我一個人失聲大哭，在深夜三點，替老王鬱怒，替老王茫然，天道怎會如此的呢？怎麼會呢？

known him for many decades. He often rode around on an old bicycle and announced his wares in a broken voice much like the sound made by his old bicycle.

"*Paotze...Mantao...ToushaPao...*"[2]

As a rule, these vendors were northerners with dark complexions, strong and solidly built, but with unhappy eyes. They usually sold plain bread, but to cater to public taste they also sold bread with sweet fillings. In the twilight hours of the day, in the alleys, in the fading light of dusk, in every city big and small, their silhouettes, seen from behind, were like identical black papercuts.

Supposing, one day while he was kneading dough, a fellow provincial brought him a letter, dirty and faded from much handling. He opened the letter. The message was simple and devastating: Mother died in 1970...

I did not know a Lao Wang, but I knew that the story was true. I shed copious tears for Lao Wang in the deep of the night. I felt his anger and his loss. How can this be the way of heaven? How can it be!

2.———Paotze *is steamed bread with meat filling.* Mantou *is plain steamed bread.* Toushapao *is a bun filled with a sweet red bean paste.*

然後，我看見老王站在黃昏的浮塵裡，一臉悲悽，我清楚看見他舉起揉麵的手去擦臉上的淚痕⋯⋯我開始一行行寫下去：

賣饅頭的老王他接到了一封信

八千里外啊，死了他的老娘親

他把饅頭揉了又揉啊，揉了又揉

他把那封信放進了他的圍裙

死了有十年啦，怪不得夢裡叫她她不應

剛蒸好的饅頭咧，娘，您就嚐嚐新

這些年賣了有多少饅頭我也數不清

為什麼偏偏不能放一個在您的掌心

清晨，我把孩子叫來，唸那首歌詞給他們聽。

「老王收到的那封信裡寫什麼，你們知道嗎？」

Then I saw him, Lao Wang, out there in the dusty mist in the evening hours, his face full of grief. I saw him clearly, lifting his hand, still covered with dough, to wipe the tears from his face... my thoughts started to fall in place; line after line I wrote:

Lao Wang the bread vendor received a letter
Eight thousand li away, ah! his old mother had passed away
He kneaded and kneaded. Ah! Kneaded and kneaded again
He taked the letter into his apron pocket
Been dead these ten years, ah!
No wonder she didn't answer his calls in his dreams
The freshly steamed buns, niang,[3] taste one while it's hot
How many I have sold these past years I've forgotten
Why is it I cannot place one in your palm?

Early the next morning I called the children to me and read them my lyric.

"Do you know what was in the letter Lao Wang received?"

3.——— *an appellation for mother in certain parts of China.*

「知道，」他們的面色平靜，有如回答一道數學題：「他媽媽死了嘛！」

然後他們急著找溜冰鞋，難得的晴冷乾爽的日子，他們要去樓下公園的溜冰場玩。

我要告訴他們老王母親在那人間地獄裡三十年的倚閭而望的苦痛嗎？我要告訴他們萬千人子在三分之一世紀以來像通緝犯等待被捕一般，等待這驚心報喪的一剎嗎？不要，讓他們笑聲如鈴，飛身下樓，和公園裡的朋友一起去溜冰吧！

&

就連我自己，孩提時不也一無所知嗎？當整個江山轟然陸沉之際，我在幹什麼呢？我在讀《愛麗

"We know," they answered in the same manner as they would a math question, their faces perfectly tranquil. "His mother died."

Then they hurried away in search of their skates. It was a rare crisp cold day. They wanted to go downstairs to the skating rink in the park.

Do I want to tell them that Lao Wang's mother had gone through thirty years of hell on earth? Do I want to describe to them how she felt as she stood by the village gate, waiting and hoping? Do I want to tell them that for a third of a century, tens of thousands of sons and daughters have been waiting for this shattering moment, waiting like criminals awaiting arrest? No, let their laughter ring like a bell; let them run down the stairs to join their friends in the park.

☙

Wasn't I, too, as ignorant as they in my younger days? What was I doing when the whole country fell with a thud? I was reading

絲》，我在每晚巴結的又搖扇子又倒茶，請寄居在我家的三舅講《西遊記》，一回一回，千山萬水，說不盡的妖魔鬼怪，專等著吃唐僧一口肉，但他卻萬水千山，一程一程走去，一心一念，只想取經……

那些年許多事都忘了，只記得下雨天，滿田埂都是紫褐色的蝸牛，我興奮的帶著鐵筷子去撿，每撿它幾十個，便送去給阿伯——阿伯是我們隔鄰的老農，他的太太便把蝸牛剁了，餵鴨子。

去年，三舅心臟病發，去世了，我趕到基隆，在釘棺前看他最後一眼，只因我還感念，那些夏夜，他怎樣跟我們講起唐僧和孫悟空、豬八戒，四面流螢中，小小的我彷彿看見唐僧一雙定定的越過大漠而直望向西方的眼睛。

Alice in Wonderland. I was ingratiating my self with my third uncle, fanning him, bringing him tea, begging him to tell me the story of the Monkey King. Chapter after chapter, over many mountains and across numerous rivers, endless numbers of goblins and demons and evil spirits were waiting to devour the priest. But he walked across those numerous mountains and endless numbers of rivers, step by step, with only one thought in mind, to get the Sutra...

It's been many years, and I have forgotten a lot, but one thing I remember: on rainy days the rice fields would be full of brownish-colored snails. I would take a container and go down to the fields to pick them up with enthusiasm. After gathering a certain number of them I would bring them to A-po, an old farmer next door. His wife would crack them and feed them to the ducks.

Last year my third uncle died of a heart attack. I rushed to Keelung to pay my last respects before the coffin was nailed shut. I was still grateful for the many stories he told us on those summer nights long ago, stories about the priest, the Monkey King, and the Pig. As the stories unfolded, little me was able to visualize Priest Tang crossing the great desert, his eyes steadily fixed towards the west, while fire-flies danced around me.

三舅的胸前堆著幾本書，一本《左傳》放在最上面，裡面還夾著一隻紅鉛筆，說是他臨終那天還在看的，我幾乎想過去搖他，請他坐起來，再為我講一段「東周列國誌」……

那段歲月，我不曾知道整個民族的悲劇，因而才勉強有一段安恬的童年。能看稻浪，能以番薯葉作耳環，能幻想自己是孫悟空的童年。而三十年過去，清風明月，何物不可悟道？花香鳥語，何處不是玄機？一部《西遊記》，一片騰騰而香的陽光下的稻田，幼小時的每一件幸福，在在都能指示我中國人的路，那鬼域中的「十年惡夢，一場浩劫」，當年不知道也罷。

A few books were placed on my third uncle's chest. The one on top was *Tso Chuan*, with a red pencil in its fold. They said he was reading it the day he died. I almost wanted to go over and shake him, asking him to sit up and tell me another episode from *The Romance of the Eastern Chou*.

In those days I was not aware of the tragedy hanging over all of us and was therefore able to enjoy a peaceful childhood. Those were the days when I stared at the waves created by the rice stalks in the fields, and those were the days when I wore potato leaves as earrings and when I dreamed that I was the Monkey King. Now thirty years have gone by. The soft breeze, the bright moon, can't they too bring us an understanding of *tao,* the truth? Isn't there magic in the fragrance of flowers and in the singing of the birds too? The book *Journey to the West*, the aroma of the steaming rice fields under the summer sun, and every other blessing of my childhood, each in its own way, can show me the way of the Chinese people. If I were unaware of the "ten long years of nightmare, and the wide cataclysmic sweep of events" which took place in the ghastly land, well, it was just as well that I was unaware of it at the time.

讓我們也帶著縱容和寵愛看著這一代的孩子吧！讓他們的笑靨補償他們祖父那一代的血淚和父親那一代的汗漿吧！至於五千年裡這慘絕的三十二年，至於這佔地一千一百萬平方公里的巨型悲劇劇場，等他們成人的時候再告訴他們吧！唯願這世上有一個詳夢者，其人有大如山的身體，深如谷的耳朵，才能一一聽取這三十二年來訴之不盡的徹骨辛酸，只有他能回答我們，為什麼這場惡夢如此緊纏密裹，猶如午夜驚汗，不能轉醒。

對於年輕的孩子，我總是給予祝福和信任。舊約裡，東征西討的憂患國王大衛，一心想為上帝建殿，上帝卻居然拒絕了，寧可選擇他的兒子所羅門——一個在安詳樂利的環境中長大的孩子。中國平劇和武俠小說裡最後總攬大局的絕不是肌肉虯結髭鬚怒張的莽夫，而是心閒氣定廓然有容的白面書生。能修得天下

Let us also look upon this generation of children with indulgence and love. Let their laughter make up for their grandfathers' blood and tears and their fathers' sweat and toil. About these thirty-two tragic years in the annals of five thousand years, and the great tragedy which took place on a huge stage of eleven million square kilometers, let us wait until they grow up before telling them! How I wish there were a Diviner of Dreams in this world, his body as large as a mountain and his ears as deep as the valleys. Only thus would he be able to absorb the innumerable, untold, bone-chilling tales of the past thirty-two years. Only he can tell us why it is that this nightmare has bound and fettered us so tightly that even when it causes us to sweat with fear at midnight we still cannot fully awaken.

To the young children I want to give my blessings and my trust, always. In the *Old Testament*, King David fought to the east and to the west with only one thought in mind: to build a place for God. But God rejected him. Instead, He picked his son, Solomon, a child who grew up in peace and happiness. In the Chinese operas and in novels about knights-errant, in the end the ones who have final control of a situation are always the fair-faced scholars who are

第一等武功的不是塵土滿面的江湖倦客，而是那純潔的一無心機的豪氣少年。

就讓他們不知道吧，就讓他們抱著吉他唱校園歌曲吧！就讓他們去爬大霸尖山吧！就讓他們穿著牛仔褲躺在陽光草坪上數流浪的雲吧！少年別無責任，就讓幸福是他們的責任吧！須知這舉世滔滔四十二億人口裡又有幾個是幸福的？世上但能多一個福人，也就是少一個苦人。苦人少而福人多不就是這一代的幸福嗎？所謂政治，所謂主義，原是我們有權利可以不懂的東西，我們只要懂一件事，我們和我們的子女必須有明天！

如果他們由於太年輕而不懂共產黨曾帶給這世界多大的災難，如果他們的眼睛還不曾透視這人類史上比一切山崩海嘯地震澇旱和饑荒更慘烈的傷口，就容

at peace with the world, not the muscle-flexing warriors with dark angry beards. Those who are able to reach perfection in the skills of martial arts are not the weary dust-covered travelers, but the heroic youths who are pure in heart.

Let them not know. Let them hold their guitars in their arms and sing their campus songs! Let them go climb Tapachien Mountain. Let them lie under the sun on the grass in their jeans and count the floating clouds. Youth has no responsibility, so just let happiness be their responsibility! How many among the world's surging population of forty-two hundred million are really lucky? One more lucky person in the world means one fewer unhappy being. Isn't this the blessing of this generation? As for politics, doctrines, and tenets, we have the right not to understand them. We need only understand one thing: there must be a tomorrow for us and our children!

If, because they are too young, they do not comprehend the fact that the communists brought a great disaster to this world, and if their eyes do not see the great big gaping wound left in human history, worse than any caused by the collapse of mountains, or

他們暫且不知道吧！少年時期的劉秀何曾知道自己要肩負多沉重的擔子。大衛在殺死巨人歌利亞之前一直是一個面頰紅潤小手不離甩石機的村野孩子。

&

難民營裡那女孩冷笑得好：

「你們，你們那裡知道什麼叫共產黨。」

不錯，我們都不算知道。但是，有一件事我們知道，總有一天，我們要讓我們的子子孫孫不再知道什麼叫共產黨。總有一天，當一個孩子拿著書本來問父親什麼叫「共產黨」的時候，得到的答覆是：「我也不清楚，你自己去查字典，反正是個很古怪、很恐怖、很荒唐的東西就是了。」

by the roaring of the angry seas, or by earthquakes, or drought, or famine, then let them be temporarily unaware of it. Did the young Liu Hsiu, first Emperor of the Later Han Dynasty, know that he was to shoulder such an awful load of responsibility? Before David killed Goliath he was merely a red-cheeked village boy who always carried a sling shot in his little hand.

80

The girl in the refugee camp was right when she laughed coldly and said, "You people! What do you know about communism?"

True, none of us really know. But one thing we do know: there will be a day when our children will know nothing about communism. There will be a day when a child will show his father the word "communism" in his book and want to know what the word means. The answer he gets will be, "I am not sure. Look it up in the dictionary yourself. Anyway, it was a strange and horrible and ridiculous thing."

　　我把那苗人的嵌著青瓷的菱形銀項鍊懸在胸前，一個貼近我心跳的位置，一時懸在胸前的東西忽然沉甸起來，那是素未謀面卻又如聞其聲的萬千族人，地理書上西南方向綿延美麗多神話的山巒，以及一夕之間成萬的被暗算而躺在山中的苗人屍體。我忽然對自己說：

　　「但，讓我知道吧！說給我聽那悽慘的情由！讓我知道更多！我已是成年人，有夠強的心肌，可以聽最傷心的故事，有夠硬的肩膀，可以挑起如山的憂患，有夠鹹的眼淚，可以為淚枯的人致哀。讓我知道吧！且讓我以今日的一番知道，換取子子孫孫億萬年永遠不必再知道那悲劇的權利吧！」

　　──原載於一九八一年三月二十九日《中國時報》，
收入九歌版《再生緣》（2010年）

ॐ

I put on the silver necklace, inlaid with blue porcelain, made by the Miao people, letting it hang near my heart. Suddenly this thing on my chest felt very heavy. It represented thousands of people whom I had never met, but whose voices seemed to be ringing in my ears. It represented what our geography books referred to as the beautiful mountain peaks in the southwest, and it also represented the thousands of bodies of the murdered Miao. All of a sudden I said to myself:

"But, let me know! Tell me the sorrowful tales. Tell me more! I am an adult now, and I have a strong heart. I can listen to the saddest of tales. I have powerful shoulders; I can carry any burden of grief. I have salty tears to shed for all those who have run dry. Let me know! With the knowledge I gain today let me be allowed to earn a right of ignorance for future generations. Let's spare our children for millions of years to come the knowledge of this tragedy.

"*The Chinese PEN*" Summer, 1984

你真好，你就像我少年伊辰

You're So Good, You're Just Like Me When I Was Young

彭安之／譯

Translated by An-Chih Perng

　　她朝我甜蜜溫婉的笑了起來——連她的笑也有蜜柑的味道——她說：「啊，你這查某真好，我知，我看就知——」我微笑，沒說話，生意人對顧客總有好話說，可是她仍抓住話題不放……「你真好——你就我少年伊辰一樣——」

她坐在淡金色的陽光裡，

面前堆著的則是一垛濃金色的柑仔。

是那種我最喜歡的圓緊飽甜的「草山桶柑」。

而賣柑者向例好像都是些老婦人，老婦人又一向都有

張風乾橘子似的臉。這樣一來，真讓人覺得她和柑仔

有點什麼血緣關似的，其實賣番薯的老人往往有點像

番薯，賣花的小女孩不免有點像花蕾。

那是一條僻靜的山徑，我停車，蹲在路邊，跟她

買了十斤柑仔。

找完了錢，看我把柑仔放好，她朝我甜蜜溫婉的

笑了起來 —— 連她的笑也有蜜柑的味道 —— 她說：

「啊，你這查某（閩南語，指女人）真好，我知，我看就

知 —— 」

我微笑，沒說話，生意人對顧客總有好話說，可

是她仍抓住話題不放……

She sat in the pale golden sunlight, facing a mound of deep golden tangerines.
It was that round, firm and sweet kind of "Grass Mountain Tankan" which I fancy most.
Tangerine vendors always seem to be some old ladies, and old ladies always have faces like wind-battered tangerines. Thus it really seems as if there were some kinship between her and the tangerines. Come to think of it, old men selling yams often look somewhat like yams, and little girls selling flowers can't help looking somewhat like flower buds.

It was a quiet and little-taken mountain trail. I stopped the car, squatted by the road, and bought six kilos of tangerines from her.

Having handed me the change and seen me put the tangerines in place, she smiled at me sweetly—even her smile had the taste of sweet tangerines—saying, "Ah, you good woman, I know, I know just by looking—"

I smiled, not saying a word. Vendors always have something nice to say to their customers, but she stuck to the subject...

「你真好──你就我少年伊辰（閩南語，指「那時候」）一樣──」

我一面趕緊謙稱「沒有啦」，一面心裡暗暗好笑起來──奇怪啊，她和我，到底有什麼是一樣的呢？

我在大學的講堂上教書，我出席國際學術會議，我駕著標緻的二〇五在山徑御風獨行。在台灣，在香港，在北京，我經過海關關口，關員總會抬起頭來說：「啊，你就是張曉風。」而她只是一個老婦人，坐在路邊，販賣她今晨剛摘下來的柑仔。她卻說，她和我是一樣的，她說得那樣安詳篤定，令我不得不相信。

轉過一個峰口，我把車停下來，望著層層山巒，慢慢反芻她的話，那袋柑仔個個沉實柔膩，我取了一個掂了掂。柑仔這種東西，連摸在手裡都有極好的感覺，彷彿它是一枚小型的液態的太陽，可食、可觸、

"You're so good—you're just like me when I was young—"

I quickly replied with a modest "nah" as I thought to myself: funny, isn't it, she and me, what on earth do we have in common?

I lecture in university halls, I participate in international academic conferences, I drive my Peugeot 205 in the mountains as if riding alone on the wind. In Taiwan, in Hong Kong, in Beijing, as I go through customs, the customs officials would always look up and say, "oh, so *you* are Show Foong Chang." And she was just an old woman, sitting by the roadside, selling tangerines she had freshly picked that morning. Yet she said she and I were the same, and with such poise and assurance that I simply had to believe her.

Turning over a peak, I pulled the car over and, gazing at the layers of mountains, I chewed over her words. That bag of tangerines was solid and tender; I took one and weighed it in my hand. Tangerines even feel great when you touch them with your hands, as if they were miniature liquid suns: edible, touchable,

可觀、可嗅。

不，我想，那老婦人，她不是說我們一樣，她是說，我很好，好到像她生命中最光華的那段時間一樣好。不管我們的社會地位有多大落差，在我們共同面對著一堆金色柑仔的時候，她看出來了，她輕易就看出來了，我們的生命基本上是相同的。我們是不同的歌手，卻重複著生命本身相同的好旋律。

少年時的她是怎樣的？想來也是個一身精力，上得山下得海女子吧？她背後山坡上的那片柑仔園，是她一寸寸拓出來的吧？那些柑仔樹，年年把柑仔像噴泉一樣從地心揮灑出來的，也是她當日一棵棵栽下去的吧？滿屋子活蹦亂跳的小孩，無疑也是她一手乳養大的？她想必有著滿滿實實的一生。而此刻，在冬日山徑的陽光下，她望見盛年的我向她走來購買一袋柑仔，她卻想賣給我她長長的一生，她和一整座山的齟齬和諒

observable, smellable.

No, I think that old lady wasn't saying that we were the same; she was saying that, I was good, as good as the most glorious time of her life. Regardless of the huge gap between our social statuses, when we face a pile of golden tangerines, she noticed—so easily noticed—that our lives are basically the same. We are different singers repeating the same good melody of life itself.

What was she like in her youth? I suppose she was also all energy, a girl able to go up the mountains and down to the seas. That tangerine orchard on the hills behind her was, I suppose, ploughed by her inch by inch. And perhaps those tangerine trees that, year by year, sprinkle tangerines out of the heart of the earth like springs were also planted tree by tree by her back then. I imagine a houseful of romping kids was no doubt also brought up by her. She must have had a full and solid life. And now, under the winter sun on the mountain trails, she saw me, in my prime, walking towards her to buy a bag of tangerines, and yet she wanted

解，她的傷痕和她的結痂。但她沒有說，她只是溫和的笑。她只是相信，山徑上恆有女子走過——跟她少年時一樣好的女子，那女子也會走出沉沉實實的一生。

我把柑仔擘開，把金船似的小瓣食了下去。柑仔甜而飽汁，我彷彿把老婦的讚許一同嚥下。我從山徑的童話中走過，我從煙嵐的奇遇中走過，我知道自己是個好女人——好到讓一個老婦想起她的少年，好到讓人想起汗水，想起困厄，想起歌，想起收穫，想起喧鬧而安靜的一生。

　　——原載一九九五年五月二十九日《中國時報》

　　收入九歌版《這杯咖啡的溫度剛好》（1996年）

to sell me her long, long life—she and a whole mountain of bickering and understanding, her wounds and her scars. But she said nothing; she just smiled gently. She just believed that, there would always be women passing through the trails—women that are as good as she was when she was young, and those women would also go through a steady and solid life.

I split the tangerine open and ate the golden boat-like segments. The tangerine tasted sweet and succulent, as if I had swallowed along with it the old lady's compliments. I passed through the fairy tales of the trails. I passed through the magical encounter in the mist. I know that I am a good woman—good enough to remind an old lady of her youth, good enough to remind people of sweet, of songs, of harvest, of a clattery but quiet life.

"The Chinese PEN" **Winter, 2002**

1230點

1230 Spots

彭鏡禧／譯

Translated by Ching-hsi Perng

　　據說有人身上穿的更值一千萬。他身上也有東西值八十萬，可惜花了這八十萬的目的是讓人「看不見」身上的東西，而不是「看見」某個東西。花了八十萬只圖個不見，這話也真是不知打哪兒說起。

說好了，要在這水池邊上等王正福的。

　　水池在醫院進口的地方，池裡養些白鵝。十年
來，在這所醫院進進出出，如果沒報到一百次，五十
次總有了。奇怪的是唐大勝從來就沒有想到來這池邊
坐坐。此刻坐下，才真的覺得是個好池子，快過年
了，天氣意外的暖和，一個小孩站在池畔餵錦鯉，他
的爸爸在一旁拍照。一個大肚子的女人在散步。另外
有個病人，坐在輪椅上由人推著，寡瘦寡瘦的，正楞
楞的看著榕樹上聒噪的麻雀。那病人倒是和氣，見人
就笑，由於兩頰消肉，那嘴角都要笑到耳朵孔裡去
了。卻不知為什麼，仍然一副悲苦相。

　　他又看了那女人一眼，大肚子的女人，不知是年
前生還是年後，還有三天就是大年夜了。如果年前
生，就屬豬，年後，就屬老鼠了。人的命都是注定
的，可惜自己親娘死得早，別說時辰是記不清了，連

It was agreed that he should wait for Wang Cheng-fu by this pond.

The pond is located at the entrance to the hospital. There are geese on the pond. In the last ten years, Tang Ta-sheng had come in and out of this hospital at least fifty times—if not a hundred. Strange to say, he had never thought of sitting by this pond. Now that he is doing so, he truly feels it is a nice pond. Chinese New Year is approaching, yet the weather is surprisingly warm. By the pond stands a boy feeding golden carps, while his father is taking pictures nearby. A pregnant woman is strolling. A thin and frail patient on a wheelchair pushed by someone gazes at the noisy sparrows in a banyan tree. The patient is rather amicable for he smiles at everyone he sees and, with his cheeks so emaciated, he seems to grin from ear to ear. Somehow, however, he looks the picture of pity.

Tang takes another look at the woman, the pregnant woman, and wonders if she will give birth before or after New Year's Day. If before, the baby will have been born in the year of the pig; if after, in the year of the rat. Man's fate is preordained. It's unfortunate that his own mother died early, for not only is he unsure of the

生日都有二個說法，爹爹說是中秋節前一天，三嬸卻說是後一天。早年，碰到事情，他就恨，如果有個八字時辰，好歹可以去問問算命先生拿個主意。這幾年，日子過得淡淡的，心情也淡淡的，像聽一齣聽熟了的戲，結局早就知道了，那命，那情節，也就可以不理它了。

據說，如果找到特別靈驗的八字先生，他就有本事倒回頭，對照你的一生，把你的八字找出來。可是現在真的不需要了。本來，半年前，倒還有件事等著拿主意，可是，今天，一腳踏出診療室，他便八成決定了，而這件事一經決定，這輩子也就再沒什麼大事了。

王正福還沒來，王正福這人怪煩人的。其實，他只不過耳朵背，六十八歲的人，耳朵背一點不算什麼，偏他這人鈍得厲害，你要是不凡事盯著他一點，

exact hour of his birth, but there are two versions of the date: Father said it was the day before Mid-autumn Festival, but Third Aunt said it was after. He used to hate it when some serious matter came up: had he known the hour of his birth and his cyclical characters, he could have at least consulted a fortune-teller. In recent years, however, as his life become dull, so did his feelings. Rather like a familiar opera whose ending one already knows, the scenario of his fate can be ignore.

It is said that a remarkably acute fortune-teller could trace back an event and, on the basis of your life to date, determine the exact time of your birth. But now there is really no need for this. Half a year ago, in fact, one thing was awaiting his decision; today, however, the moment he stepped out of the doctor's office, his mind was almost made up. And once this matter is settled, nothing serious can happen for the rest of his life.

Wang Cheng-fu has not come yet. He is quite annoying. He is actually a little hard of hearing; nothing serious in a sixty-eight-year-old man. But he is so dumb that one has to mind him all the time, or he will even forget to eat. A lot of Chinese characters were

他真能連飯也忘了吃。王正福身上的字多，今天是他第一次來打，怕不要打五百點，自己第一次就打了五百四十八點，護士小姐嘴巴甜，趕著叫「伯伯」長，「伯伯」短的。

「伯伯呀，」她說：「你賺到啦，五百四十八點，都是退輔會出錢，要是自己出，每一點要一百一十二元，你今天一天就要付出六萬多哩！」

他苦笑了一下，小姐太年輕，沒法向她解釋，這種賺，誰要？民國四十二年的事了，別說這小姐沒生，就連她老娘生出來沒有都成問題，她懂什麼？

五百四十八點，一點一點都是疼，那醫生形容說，不疼不疼，就像橡皮筋彈一下，好吧，就算像橡皮筋彈一下，一連彈你五百四十八下也夠受吧？那醫

tattooed on Wang's body; so, on this first day of treatment, he was to have at least five hundred spots removed. Tang himself got five hundred and forty-eight the first time. The nurse had a sweet way of cajoling, calling him "Uncle" all the time.

"Uncle," she said, "you're in luck! All these five hundred and forty-eight spots were paid for by the VACRS.[1] If you had to pay for them yourself, each spot being worth one hundred and twelve NT dollars, it would cost sixty grand or more for today's treatment alone!"

He forced a smile. The nurse was so young there was no use explaining to her: who needs this kind of luck? It all happened in 1953. Maybe even her mother was not born yet, let alone herself. What did she know?

Five hundred and forty-eight laser spots, and every one of them hurt. The doctor compared it to the sting from a snapping rubber band. All right, so it's like being snapped by a rubber band; to be snapped five hundred and forty-eight times at a stretch is sure to

1.——— *VACRS is Vocational Assistance Commission for Retired Servicemen.*

生也是個後生家，笑嘻嘻的：「從前刺下去才疼咧！現在除下來應該小意思啦！」

奇怪，也許那時候年輕，刺下去好像也不怎麼痛，三個針，綁成一小把，沾上黑墨，就這麼往肉裡扎。

「殺朱拔毛」那是左臂。

「反共抗俄」那是右臂。

前胸，則是一塊地圖，外加一面大旗。後背，是「不成功便成仁」。

下午的陽光暖暖的，白鵝優游，他數了一下，一共九隻，池邊杜鵑花叢下面還有幾隻，他弄不清楚牠們的數目。但不知為什麼，有一隻孤零零的綠頭鴨子夾在白鵝中間竄游，落了單，顯得十分奇怪。

hurt. The doctor was also a youngster, all smiles: "It hurt more when you got your tattoos. To have then removed should be no big deal."

Strangely—maybe because he was young then—the tattooing didn't seem to hurt much. Three pins, bunched together, were dipped into dye and pricked the skin.

"Kill Zhu and Weed out Mao" on the left arm.

"Anti-Communist; Anti-Russia" on the right arm.

On the chest was a map and a large flag; on the back, "Succeed or Die."

The afternoon sun is warm. The white geese glide leisurely. He counts nine of them, but there are several others under the azalea trees by the pond, so he isn't sure about their number. Somehow, a lonely mallard dashes and roams among them—a bizarre picture.

一陣風過，雀榕樹飄下一陣落葉。

他想起自己昨天勸王正福的話：

「不疼，也不難過，雷射，紅寶石雷射，人家美國人的科學發明！不得了的！一台機器四百多萬哪！你不去打那真錯過了天大的好機會，又不要錢，又不疼，打完了，擦點藥，三天就能洗澡，你個王正福別死腦筋了，這事如果不是好事，我會來勸你？我自己打了十一次了，明天我去打第十二次，就算功德圓滿了。好，我也幫你掛了號，你好好去打了，明年也好回老家，沒有人敢找你麻煩，不疼的，哪個龜兒子騙你？打完了，像落了幾點白白的梅花點，真的不疼的。」

其實當然還是疼的，尤其是前心後背，比手上要疼得多。但王正福這人死心眼，別人都回去了，偏他膽小，不敢回去。有時想家想狠了，就抱著信哭：

A breeze blows, and leaves whirled down from the banyan tree.

He remembers his advice to Wang Cheng-fu yesterday:

"It doesn't hurt, and it's not ugly. Laser, Ruby Laser. Scientific invention of the Americans! Remarkable! One machine costs over four million NT dollars! What a great opportunity! It's free, and it doesn't hurt. After the treatment—you rub on some medication, and in three days you can take a shower. Wang Cheng-fu, don't be stubborn. If this weren't something good, would I urge it on you? I myself have been through eleven treatments. Tomorrow I'll go for the twelfth, and then I will have come full circle. Even the appointment I've made it for you. Be good and go for the treatment, and when you return to your native land next year, nobody will give you any trouble. Doesn't hurt—I'll be damned if I lie. After the treatment, it looks like a few plum-shaped white dots have fallen on you. It really doesn't hurt."

In fact, it hurts, of course, and much more on the chest and the back than on the arms. But Wang Cheng-fu is the stubborn type. While everyone else has gone back to the mainland, he dared not go. Sometimes, when homesick enough, he would cry over the letter:

「不行啊，共產黨，說翻臉就翻臉的呀，我這一身有七面國旗，還加上『堅持反共信念，矢志雪恥復國』，還加上『八個圖台灣』，他們饒得了我？」

王正福這人現在看來顛三倒四，想不到他當年竟在臂上刺英文，他英文大字一個不識，居然還刺了英文字！唉，說起這個王正福，笑話可多了。有一次，不知怎的，長褲腳裡竟拖出二團白白的東西，仔細一看，原來是衛生褲。他說他一早明明先套衛生褲才穿外褲的，卻套了個空，等發現的時候已經是中午了。那天唐大勝一早去結匯，孫子要娶媳婦，他匯了二百美金。等回來，才發現王正福丟人現眼。他有點生氣，卻也說不上來該把王正福怎麼辦。

這種人，想當年，居然得風氣之先，刺起英文字，「八個圖台灣」據說就是「回台灣」（Back to

"But no, I can't. The communists are ever so treacherous. I have on me seven national flags, plus 'Persist in Anti-Communist Conviction; Determined to Revenge and Recover Lost Country,' plus 'Ba-ge-tu-tai-wan,' How can they forgive me?"

Wang appeared somewhat deranged, but little did Tang think that he would have some English tattooed at the time. Wang cannot even read the alphabet, and he was tattooed with some English words! Ai! This Wang Cheng-fu—he is the butt of many jokes. One time, from each of his trouser legs was pulled some white stuff, which, upon examination, turned out to be long-legged tight cotton underwear. He said he was quite sure that in the morning he had put on the underwear before he put on his trousers, but obviously he had missed. And it was already noon when he discovered the slip. Early that morning, Tang went to send two hundred US dollars to his grandson, who was getting married. Upon his return, he found Wang had become a laughing stock. He was irritated, but he did not know what to do with this man.

That such a man should, years ago, have been among the first to be tattooed with the English words! "Ba-ge-tu-tai-wan," they

Taiwan）的意思。唐大勝想到這裡，不禁好笑起來。這王正福有本事把一切的話說成四川話，包括英文，包括台語粗口。八個圖台灣也不知本來唸成什麼？

這王正福還不來，不知他今天打了幾點，他那人怕疼，自己只好多事，去關照醫生，今天先打他兩臂就可以了，前心後背留著下次再打吧！快過年了，讓他過個好年。

自己第一次也是打手，五百四十八點，隔了一個月第二次來打前心後背，六百八十二點，以後就每一個月來一次，一次打前，一次打後，他牢牢的記住了，原來自己這一身刺青全部算來是一千二百三十點，換成新台幣，是十三萬七千七百六十元，各打六次，一共是八十二萬六千五六十元。

say, means "Back to Taiwan." Tang cannot help laughing when he thinks of this. Wang Cheng-fu has the gift to turn every language—including English and irreverent Taiwanese—into Szechwanese. How does one say "Ba-ge-tu-tai-wan" in English, Tang wonders.

Wang had still not shown up. Tang is curious to know how many laser spots he's got today. As Wang dreads pain, Tang took it upon himself to remind the doctor only do Wang's two arms today, leaving the chest and the back for next time. It's close to New Year; let him have a nice holiday.

Tang's own first treatment was on the arms too. Five hundred and forty-eight spots. A month later, during the second treatment on the chest and back, he received six hundred and eighty-two spots. After that, he has come once a month, treating in turn the chest or the back. He kept it firmly in mind: he had altogether one thousand two hundred and thirty little holes. Translated into money, it comes to one hundred and thirty-seven thousand seven hundred and sixty NT dollars. With each hole treated six times, the cost amounts to eight hundred and twenty-six thousand five hundred and sixty dollars.

「我這也是有了身價的人了，我這一身『沒有』，也值一百萬哩——這是在榮總，要是去美容院打，一點要五百元，那就是四百萬啦。」

報上有時看到綁架的新聞，綁匪動不動要三、五百萬或幾千萬，他實在想不通一個人怎麼可以值那麼多錢！

活到六十九歲，嘿！這輩子就是現在最值錢。刺上青，並沒有讓自己值錢，但這一除青，卻除掉了一百萬，哈，人生凡事都是注定的。

聽說有位老兄刺了一身正氣歌，也去打，真不知他打了幾點，那人贏回的一身白皮肉，少說也值三百萬。奇怪的是，正氣歌幹麼要打呢？文天祥哪一點得罪共產黨了？

"I am thus a man of wealth. This 'nothing' on my body is worth close to a million dollars—at the rate of the Veterans General Hospital. In a beauty parlor, they charge five hundred per spot, which means four million in total!"

Occasionally news about kidnappings appeared in the paper. The kidnappers often demand three to five million dollars or even tens of millions. He has never understood how a person can be worth that much.

At the age of sixty-nine—now! He has never in all his life been so valuable! The tattooing itself did not enhance his worth, but its removal costs a million dollars. Ha! Everything in life is preordained.

He's heard of a chap with the "Song of Righteousness" tattooed all over his body, who also went for its removal. He wonders how many prickings that man had to endure. The fair skin he got in return must be worth at least three million dollars. What he cannot understand is why the "Song of Righteousness" should be removed. How could its author Wen Tien-hsiang[A.D.1236-82] have offended the communists?

四十多年前咬牙忍受針扎之痛的當時，誰會想到老來還有這一劫呢？唉，人生沒啥理可說，一切都是老天注定的。

那一年，打韓戰，三十九年，六月二十五。自己是十月才去的，手裡一把漢陽造，居然還是國軍當年的舊貨。槍還來不及開，美軍的大砲就轟過來，人就這樣被俘了。

兩方交換戰俘，奇怪的是，五個中國戰俘換一個美國戰俘。那是他第一次知道，美國人是值錢的，和中國人比，一個抵五個。

中國人命不值錢！韓戰戰場上二十幾的、三十幾的一個個都死了。那些小的才十五、六歲，訓練三個月，會一點劈刺，就開上陣去。天知道，肉搏訓練根本使不上力啊，美軍只打長距離的仗，誰會送個身

Forty-odd years ago, when they courageously endured the pain of piercing pins, who would have expected this ill luck in old age? Ai, there is no reasoning out this life. There's providence in everything.

The Korean War broke out on the 25th of June, 1950. Tang went in October with a rifle made by Han-yang Arsenal—junk from the Nationalist Army days. He had not yet had the chance to fire a shot when the American shells boomed and he was captured.

The two sides exchanged POWs. What puzzled him was that five Chinese POWs would be exchanged for one U. S. POW. For the first time it occurred to him that Americans were worth more: they were five to one against the Chinese.

Lives of the Chinese were worthless! In the battlefields of the Korean War, soldiers in their twenties and thirties died one on top of the other. The youngest were only fifteen or sixteen. After three months' training and barely able to manage the bayonet, they were driven to the battlegrounds. God only knew that hand-to-hand

體過來跟你肉搏。殺——嘿——殺——嘿——嘿嘿嘿——殺——嘿，誰跟你玩這個？

一塊彈片飛過來，嵌在背肉裡，取出來，留下碗口大個疤，韓戰對他來說，就是這麼多了，碗口大的記憶。

一個人到底值多少錢呢？

怎麼有人值一億呢？可是綁匪開的就是這價錢。

據說有人身上穿的便值一千萬。他身上也有東西值八十萬，可惜花了這八十萬的目的是讓人「看不見」身上的東西，而不是「看見」某個東西。花了八十萬只圖個不見，這話也真是不知打哪兒說起。

combat drills were of no avail, since the Americans only fought from a distance. They never sent people over for hand-to-hand combat. Thrust!—Hey!—Thrust!—Hey!—Hey—Hey—Hey!—Thrust!—Hey,who's going to use the bayonet?

Shrapnel flew his way and pierced his back. It was taken out, leaving a scar the size of a rice bowl. For him, that was all the Korean War—memories the size of a rice bowl.

How much is a person worth, after all?

How can some people be worth a hundred million dollars? But that's the price some kidnappers ask.

They say some people's dress is worth ten million. He also has something on him that's worth eight hundred thousand. Unfortunately, that eight hundred thousand was spent so that people *cannot see* the thing on him, not so that they can *see* it. Eight hundred thousand dollars for something not to be seen—he cannot begin to explain it.

聽說林彪跟毛澤東交惡就在韓戰以後，韓戰死了不少人，大概是兩百萬吧？剩下的人極少。他自己那一連一百八十人全死光，就剩他一個。回去以後，毛澤東居然對林彪發火：

「幹麼帶人回來？我打韓戰就是要消滅中國人口，幹麼不打得死光光？」

把左臂刺上「殺朱拔毛」，對他來說，是心甘情願的。

「怎麼啦？不反共了啊？」

年輕的醫生嘻嘻哈哈的跟他開玩笑，也許是為了讓病人輕鬆一點吧，他想。

「不用我來反，」唐大勝篤篤定定：「他們自己一個個都窩裡反了！」

「也不殺朱拔毛嗎？咦？毛是毛澤東，朱又是誰

They say that it is after the Korean War that Lin Biao fell afoul of Mao Zedong. Many people died in the War—perhaps two million. Very few survived. In his company, all of the 180 but him died. After the war, to everyone's surprise, Mao got mad at Lin:

"Why bring people back? I fought the Korean War in order to annihilate the Chinese population. Why not fight until everyone has died?"

To have his left arm tattooed "Kill Zhu and Weed out Mao" was his wish.

"Why, no longer Anti-Communist?"

The young doctor joked with him lightly, perhaps to make his patient relax a bit, Tang thought.

"There's no need for me to fight against them," he said with confidence. "They're fighting against each other now!"

"And no more Kill Zhu and Weed out Mao, either? Well, Mao

啊？」

「朱是朱德，當時的總司令。」他說：「現在也不用我來動手殺了，他們都自己去閻王爺那裡報到了，倒省得我麻煩。」

醫生戴個金絲邊眼鏡，娃娃臉，望著不過二十出頭，這小龜娃兒（按：四川人罵人龜姓、龜兒並無惡意）又懂什麼來著。

他從不肯說一句委屈這一身刺青的話，不像鄭家孝。

鄭家孝有一次在國父紀念館，正看人放風箏，不知怎麼的碰上一個民進黨，民進黨拉住他，說：

「喂，你這『反共抗俄』的，你待在台灣幹什麼？去呀，去呀，去反攻大陸嘛！站在這裡吃台灣的米幹麼？」

means Mao Zedong. but who's this Zhu?"

"Zhu means Zhu De, then their Commander-in-Chief," he said. "There's no need for me to kill them now. They've both reported to Yama. [2] Saved me the trouble."

The doctor wore a pair of gold-rimmed glasses. He had a baby face, looked just over twenty. What does this little brat know?

Tang would never say anything to disgrace his tattoos. Unlike Cheng Chia-hsiao.

One day, Cheng was watching people fly kites on the grounds of Sun Yat-sen Memorial Hall when he came across a member of the Democratic Progressive Party (DPP). The latter stopped him and asked:

"Hey you, you the 'Anti-Communist and Anti-Russia,' what are you doing in Taiwan? Go, go and recover your Mainland! Why do you stand here and eat Taiwan's rice?"

2.———Yama *is the name of the judge of the underworld in Chinese folklore.*

鄭家孝給扯急了，就反吼回去：

「我又不是自願刺的，是強迫的！人家迫我刺的。」

他有點氣鄭家孝，沒出息，民進黨又能他媽的把你怎麼樣，何況他臉上又沒刺字，你怎麼知道他是民進黨？就算是民進黨又怎麼樣？民進黨也不能管你自家刺自家皮肉呀！更何況當年如果不反共不抗俄，大家全成了毛主席的順民，還容得下你這批小王八蛋如今在這裡撐米脹飯滿口胡言哩！

從前，自己這批人，這一萬四千人，有個名堂，叫「反共義士」。還拍過電影，叫《一萬四千個證人》。剛回台灣那天還披紅掛彩遊行，到處萬人空巷。如今，谷正綱一死，「一・二三，自由日」也沒人過了。講，也沒人演了。這還不說，居然光天化日之下，又在堂堂國父紀念館前面，也會冒出這種小烏

Pulling away, Cheng shouted back:

"I didn't do it of my own free will. They forced it on me! They forced me to be tattooed."

Tang is somewhat angry at Cheng. That good-for-nothing! What could the damned DPP member have done to you anyway? Besides, he had no tattoo on his face; how could you know he was a DPP member? And even if he was, so what? What was it to the DPP if you wanted to pierce your own skin? Moreover, if we had not fought the communists in those years, we would have all ended up as subjects of Chairman Mao. Would you sons of bitches then be able to talk such nonsense with your stomachs full?

In the days gone by, fourteen thousand of us had a title: "Anti-Communist Freedom Seekers." A movie was made of our story, entitled *Fourteen Thousand Witnesses*. On the day of our arrival in Taiwan, we were decorated with colorful silk stripes and paraded. There was a large turnout everywhere we went. Now, as soon as Ku Cheng-kang died, the 1-23 Freedom Day goes unobserved.[3] Speeches are no longer given. Moreover, in front of the memorial

---

3.———*Ku Cheng-kang was in his lifetime a staunch anti-communist who presided over many a ceremony in celebration of Freedom Day, which falls on January 23rd (1-23 for short).*

龜王八蛋來，真他媽的嘔人！更嘔人的是家孝這種孬貨，居然說自己是遭人強迫的，也真是丟人丟到家了。鄭家孝，你先人板板！

「你當年是志願的嗎？還是強迫的？」他嚇了一跳，怎麼醫生會問這種問題？那是他第二次去打雷射，一面胸膛正被那一張國旗扯得麻辣火燒。他聞到微微的肉焦味，他忽然想到那味道有幾分熟悉。回一下神，才想到這是當年戰場上的味道，火燒皮肉，就是這種味道。

原來那場韓戰打到現在還在善後，原來四十四年之後才是尾聲。

「也不能說是強迫的。」他回答醫生，胸口一陣疼過一陣，「人家一萬四千人都刺了，你一個人不刺，好意思嗎？」

hall of our nation's founding father should turn up in broad daylight that mother-fucking whoreson! Damned disgusting! Even more disgusting is the incredible fact that the good-for nothing Cheng Chia-hsiao should say that he was forced. This is the greatest of scandals! Cheng Chia-hsiao, fuck your shameless ancestors!

"Were you willing then, or were you coerced?" Tang was surprised that the doctor should ask such a question. That was the second time he went for the laser treatment. His chest was being torn and heated by the national flag. He could smell a slight burning, and all of a sudden he found the smell familiar. Recovering himself, he realized that it was the smell of the battlefield in the past; flesh scorched by fire—that was the smell.

So the Korean War had continued to this day for its finale; the epilogue was taking place forty-four years later.

"I wouldn't say I was forced," he replied, his chest hurting more and more. "Fourteen thousand have been tattooed. Wouldn't it have been a shame not to go along?"

「哦，」醫生扶了扶他的藍眼罩，因為怕雷射光，他打點的時都戴著副藍眼罩，像電視上的蝙蝠俠什麼的「這麼說來，是『同儕壓力』。」

「什麼同才？」他聽不懂，「我們是『同袍』。」

「同儕，人字邊一個齊，就是同夥人的意思，同儕彼此會形成一種約束力。」

醫生看來有點學問，醫生的話他半懂不懂，也不想深究。胸口疼得厲害，叫疼，是不作興的，太娘娘腔了，但眼角畢竟還是微微滲出了淚水。

上一次流淚是五年前的事了，那是他第一次回老家，知道他在台灣沒娶，女人走了二十里路來看他。一進門，就直蹶蹶的跪下了。

"Ah," said the doctor, adjusting the blue eye-shield he wore to protect himself from the laser beams while operating—rather like Batman or something on TV. "So it's 'peer pressure.'"

"What beer?" he didn't understand. "We had no beer then."

"Peer. People of the same group. They form a binding force among themselves."

The doctor seemed to have some learning. What he said Tang could only half-comprehend and he had no intention to delve into the subject. It hurt a lot on the chest, but you're not supposed to scream—that would be too womanish. But from the corner of his eyes seeped some tears, after all.

The previous occasion he shed tears was five years ago. the first time he returned to his native home. When his wife learned that he had not remarried in Taiwan, she walked twenty kilometers to meet him. No sooner had she entered the door than she dropped upon her knees:

「沒能給你守著，是我對不住你——」

扶不起人來，他只好也跪下。

「快別說這話了，我謝都來不及，一兒一女，都這麼大了——連孫子都有了，也多虧你一人扛。」

他送女人一條雞心鍊子，女人沒收也沒拒，只說：「我不方便，我戴著，那邊的會多心。還是給小紅吧，看見小紅戴著，就好比我自己戴著一樣，我嫁你那年，也是十八。」

小紅是他們的孫女，活脫脫是女人的當年。

那以後，他就沒再流過淚。

那時候是晚春，穿長袖襯衫，倒也不熱，手上的字，也就掩過去了。到了晚上，去灶下洗澡，三弟為

"I have not remained your wife, I have let you down—"

Unable to make her stand up, he had to kneel down also:

"Leave off such talk. I'm more than grateful to you—our son and daughter are both grown up—and there's even a grandson. I'm indebted to you for shouldering the responsibility alone."

He gave his wife a heart-shaped necklace. She neither accepted nor declined it, but simply said:"It's inconvenient for me. If I wear it the other side might be suspicious. Rather give it to Xiao-hong. To see Xiao-hong wear it is like wearing it myself. I was also eighteen when I married you."

Xiao-hong is their granddaughter, the exact picture of his wife when she was young.

After that he had not shed tears.

It was late spring. It was not too hot to wear long-sleeved shirt, and in this way he was able to cover up the characters on his

他倒水，灶間燈暗，只有五燭光吧。

「哎呀！」三弟叫起來：「二哥，你這背上怎麼花胡離拉的！」

沒料到他眼尖，他只好照實說了，三弟也是個小幹部，聽了那番話竟有點作難起來：「這玩意兒，說嚴重嘛不嚴重——說不嚴重嘛說不定也有點嚴重。自家人看到了也就罷了，要是外人看了，怕不有麻煩！我看，還是小心點，『共產黨像月亮』——這句話你聽過吧？——『初一十五不一樣』。」

那以後，他就沒回去過。

王正福不知搞什麼鬼，打到現在還不出來。

arms. In the evening, he went to the kitchen to take a bath. His third younger brother poured water for him. The dim light in the kitchen was only about five watts.

"Oh my!" his brother exclaimed. "Second Elder Brother, whatever happened to your back—such a messy color?"

Tang didn't expect his brother to be so sharp-eyed, and he had to tell the truth. Third Brother is a low-ranking cadre. When he heard it he looked troubled: "This thing is not serious—but then it can be somewhat serious. It's alright for family members to see it, but if it is seen by others, there will be trouble. I think we ought to be careful. 'Communists are like the moon'—you've heard the expression?—'they are different on the first day and on the fifteenth of the mouth.'"

Since then, he had not returned to his Mainland home.

What the hell is with Wang Cheng-fu? Is he not finished with the treatment?

兒子寫信來，要他回去長住，他認真的考慮了一年，決定先打雷射除了刺青再說。

這王正福人是鈍了一點，好在膽子小，還不致出大毛病。不像黎志新，差點沒弄出人命來。那是八、九年前的事了，他不知聽誰說的，找了個女子美容院的老闆娘，弄了些燙頭髮的藥料，就這樣腐蝕起自己的皮膚來。結果字沒除掉，皮膚弄得潰爛紅腫，慘不忍睹，挨了醫官一頓好罵。

另外還有個勞久忠，這人也是異想天開。那也是十年前的事了，他想家想瘋了，那時候又沒這雷射好打，他找了個紋身店，把那些字紛紛改刺成青龍。為了將就那些字那些圖形，刺的龍當然不會好看，有那缺德的人就給他取個外號叫「九龍壁」，也有人叫他「怪龍壁」，後來終於定了案，叫「勞九龍」，大概因為跟勞久忠沾點關係。那勞久忠的龍他看過，因

Tang's son wrote him a letter, asking him to go home for good. Having given it serious consideration for a year, he decided to have the tattoo removed by laser first.

Wang Cheng-fu is a little on the dumb side. Luckily, he is also somewhat timid and has caused no big trouble, unlike Li Chih-hsiu who almost got himself killed. That was eight or nine years ago. On someone's advice he went to the proprietor of a beauty parlor and got hold of material used for perms. With it he corroded his own skin. As a result, the characters still remained, but his skin was all burns and welts. It was a terrible sight. Li was severely reprimanded by the medical officer.

And then there is Lao Chiu-chung, another person of fantastical notions. It happened also about ten years ago. He missed his native home so much he almost went crazy, but back then there was no such thing as laser treatment. So he went to a tattoo shop to turn the Chinese characters into green dragons. Having to fit in with the original characters, however, the dragons did not look good. Mischievous tongues played on his name, nicknaming him "Lao Chiu-lung," which means "Lao the Dragons," punning on "Lousy

為刺成一團，胡亂糾結，到底有幾條也分不清。不過，他畢竟去了老家，這兩年他兒子還過來探親哩！勞九龍畢竟也來打雷射了，中間還費了點唇舌。人家退輔會出錢幫忙除青，除的是「忠黨愛國」「解救大陸」，從來沒見過來除龍的。頗經過一番解釋，又請部隊長出面說明，才弄懂他那一群龍的來龍去脈。只是半路上平白又多刺了那麼多點，現在也只好多打，痛得他咬牙切齒，一面胸膛打滿了，黑壓壓的，像戴了一面護心鏡似的。

　　「勞先生呀，」醫生開他玩笑，「你刺的這滿身龍，倒像參加了什麼幫派哩，你是青幫洪幫？」

　　「大夫呀！我們當年參的那個幫規矩可嚴哩！」這勞九龍讀過中學，腦筋轉得快，「我們不刺不准入幫，我們那個幫不是青幫洪幫，叫國民黨幫。」

Dragons." Tang has seen Lao's dragons, but because they are all contorted and mixed up, he does not know how many there are. But at least Lao has returned home; his son had even come and visited him in Taiwan! After a while Lao received laser treatment, but it required a bit of persuasion. The VACRS has been subsidizing the removal of such tattoos as "Loyalty to Party and Country" and "Liberate the Mainland," but is has never seen tattooed dragons. It was only with much explanation and even the personal testimony of Lao's former commanding officer that the origin of his dragons was clarified. Since the number of his punctures had increased, he now had to endure more laser spots which hurt him so much that he clenched his teeth tightly. After the treatment, the dark chest looked as if covered with a protective plate.

"Mr. Lao," the doctor said jokingly, "with these dragons all over your body , you look like a gangster. Are you a member of the Ching Pang or the Hung Pang?"

"Doctor, the gang we joined in those days had very strict rules," replied Lao. Lao had had middle school education, and possessed a quick mind. "We had to be tattooed in order to join. And our gang

勞九龍回來還把這故事說給大夥兒聽。

王正福還不來，唐大勝卻坐累了，只好站起來動動，也不敢走遠。不知不覺，他唱起一首歌來，打著四川調子：

老也好，小也好，
不老不小不得了。

唱完他逕自笑了，不知怎的，竟會想起四十多年前抓兵的歌來。所謂老，是指四、五十歲，所謂小，是指十三、十四歲。至於他那時才二十三歲，正是不老不小最「不得了」的年齡，當然是非抓不可。

老也好，小也好，
不老不小不得了。

is neither the Ching Pang nor the Hung Pang, but is called the KMT."

When Lao returned from the treatment, he told the story to everyone.

Wang Cheng-fu is still not here. Tang Ta-sheng, tired of sitting, stands up and moves around. He dares not go far, however, and soon finds himself singing a song on a Szechwan tune:

The old don't have to care,
The young don't have to care,
The in-between alone
Are given the scare.

At the end of his song, he laughs—to have remembered the conscription song of more than forty years ago! "The old" refers to those aged from forty to fifty, and "the young" refers to those aged thirteen and fourteen. He was twenty-three then ,exactly one of the "in-betweens" and scared to death. He was of course conscripted.

The old don't have to care,
The young don't have to care,

也許心情還好，他又唱了一遍。正在這時候，一個清瘦的中年人走過，塞給他一疊傳單：

「伯伯，總統選林郝，國代選新黨。拜託，拜託。」

他吃了一驚，咦，這裡是榮總，是國民黨的地盤，怎麼冒出個新黨來？

他一時還沒有回過神，卻見王正福縮頭縮腦的在張望。

「我在這裡呀！」他大聲叫嚷。

這王正福是個五短身材，一聽見聲音喜得眉花眼笑，兩隻小短腿划呀划的直往這邊奔來。

The in-between alone
Are given the scare.

Maybe because he feels good, he sings the song again. At this moment, a slender middle-aged man comes along and gives him a set of leaflets:

"Sir, Lin and Hau for President and VP; New Party for the National Assembly, please. Thank you."

Tang is taken by surprise. What? This is the Veterans General Hospital, the stronghold of the KMT. How come this New Party member turns up here?

He is still wondering when he sees Wang Cheng-fu looking around timidly.

"I'm here!" he shouted.

Wang Cheng-fu is a short guy. When he hears Tang's voice he turns all smiles, and waddles on his two short legs toward Tang.

「也不算疼，可也不算不疼哩！」難得，這句話他倒說得清楚，「大夫說，你好，你混畢業啦，你不用再來啦，你下個月就一身細皮白肉啦！我完了，我才開始，我有的罪受哩！」

兩人走到門口，要去搭公車回三峽，轉白雞。

唐大勝心裡一陣空虛，像是肚子餓，又像頭昏，然而都不是。

什麼都沒了，他忽然明白。「殺朱拔毛」沒了，「反共抗俄」沒了，地圖沒了，國旗沒了，「不成功便成仁」也沒了……從今以後什麼都毀了跡，彷彿戴了四十年的戒指一旦除下，便只剩指頭上一圈白痕。空空洞洞的白。一無所有的白。

那些血淋淋的誓詞都去了哪裡呢？大夫說是鈣化

"It didn't hurt much, but it hurt!" How rare for Wang to utter a clear sentence. "The doctor says you're OK now, you've graduated, you don't have to come any more. Next month you'll have new delicate skin on you! But I'm undone, my suffering is only just beginning!"

The two of them make for the gate, to take the bus to San-hsia, where they will transfer to Pai-chi.

Tang has a feeling of hollowness. Something like an empty stomach or dizzy head. But it's neither.

Everything's gone, he suddenly realizes. Gone is "Kill Zhu and Weed out Mao," gone is "Anti-Communist and Anti-Russia," gone is the map, gone is the national flag, gone is "Succeed or Die,"...From now on everything is wiped out, as if a ring worn for forty years were suddenly removed, leaving nothing but a circle of whiteness. Whiteness of complete emptiness. Whiteness of complete nothingness.

Where are those blood-dripping oaths? The doctor says they are

了，吸收了，吸收了又是去了哪裡呢？血裡嗎？髓裡嗎？

下意識的，他又去摸摸背上那塊碗口大的疤，疤還在，糾結如樹皮，他安了點心。

「大夫叫我再過二個月來，」王正福今天不知為什麼，嘰嘰呱呱，說個不休，也許疼狠了就不那麼鈍了，「那時候，你大概回去長住囉，不過我都記下了，下次怎麼轉車，我都記住啦。」

他說得自己像個乖孩子。

他們剛好走到車站，兩人爬上車，車一時還沒開，他大聲的湊在王正福耳邊叫道：

「下次呀──我還陪你來！」

「什麼？」王正福也大聲回話：「不是說好過了

calcified, absorbed. But where do they go after absorption? Into the blood, or the marrow?

Subconsciously, he touches the bowl-size scar. It's still there, knotted like the bark of a tree. He feels a little more secure.

"The doctor tells me to come in two months," says Wang Cheng-fu. Somehow he has become a chatterbox today and would not cease talking. Maybe one is less dumb when hurting. "By then you'll probably be gone to the mainland for good. But I've got everything memorized—how to make the transfer next time, and everything."

He speaks like a good boy.

They get on the bus at the stop. Before the bus starts, Tang gets closer to Wang and shouts in his ear:
"Next time—I'll come with you again!"

"What?" Wang shouts back. "Didn't you say you would go

「『長住』的話，就以後再說吧！我想通了，我下個月回去看他們一趟，給他送點安家費就好，我過它十天就回來。我今天都想過了，這些日子，就留在三峽過就好——反正回那邊也是三峽嘛，留這裡也有三峽。哦，對了，你要給我記清楚，三峽就是底站，三峽下來轉白雞、白雞下來走路，到榮民之家。別忘了。」

「你放心。我忘不了——三峽就是底站。」

車開了，兩人都累了，並且兩人身上都有一點奇怪的疼。王正福右臂上的「八個圖台灣」抵著唐大勝左臂已經消失殆盡的「殺朱拔毛」，在車子顛簸的律動中，兩隻胳膊一路磨蹭著，而兩人也終於頭並頭的一路睡著了。

——原載一九九六年四月十四、十五日《聯合報》

home and stay with your grandson for good?"

"We'll talk about 'staying for good' later. I know what to do now. Next month I'll go visit them, and give them my family support allowance. I'll return in ten days. I've thought it all out. The rest of my life I'll just stay in San-hsia—over there it's called San-xia, and here it's also San-hsia. Oh, yes, you must remember clearly that San-hsia is the last stop, from there you transfer to Pai-chi. Get off at Pai-chi and walk to Veteran's Home. Don't forget!"

"Don't worry, I won't forget—San-hsia is the last stop."

The bus moves. Both men are tired, and both feel a strange pain. The "Ba-ge-tu-tai-wan" on Wang Cheng-fu's right arm leans against the completely erased "Kill Zhu and Weed out Mao" on Tang Ta-sheng's left arm. To the rhythmical rocking of the bus, the two arms rub against each other all the way. Finally, their heads resting on each other, the two men fall asleep.

"The Chinese PEN" **Autumn, 1996**

我撿到了一張身分證

Finding An ID

康士林／譯

Translated by Nicholas Loss

彷彿是一場「自我追尋」的心理遊戲，卻碰了壁。我找不到「我」了，「我」消失了。更可怕的是，「我」可能淪落了。

這才開始悲傷起來，聽說有人專盜人家身分證去冒用，我的不必盜，只消撿就可以了。被冒用的身分證會變成什麼下場呢？

似乎，事情如果不帶三分荒謬，就不足以言人生。

　　有個朋友Ｙ，明明是很好的水墨畫家，卻有幾分邋遢習性，畫作上不知怎的就會滴上幾點不經意而留下的墨跡，設計家Ｗ評此事，說：

　　「嗯，這好，以後鑑定他的畫就憑這個，不滴幾滴墨點的，就不算真跡。」

　　聖人的生命裡充滿聖蹟，偉人的生命裡寫滿了勳業，但凡人的生命則如我那位朋友的畫面，一方面縱橫著奇筆詭墨，一方面卻總要滴上幾滴無奈的濃濃淡淡的黑墨點子。

　　就像黑子是太陽的一部分，墨點也必須被承認為畫面的一部分。噯！我且來說說我近日生活中的一滴

It seems if there's not a tinge of preposterousness to something, it's really not worthwhile to be considered human.

A friend of mine—let's call him "Y" –is without a doubt a very fine calligraphic artist, but he has one messy habit. On his pictures, for some reason unknown to me, he seems unintentionally to make some black splotches. The designer "W" evaluates them in this way: "Indeed, this is very good. In the future, his work will be recognized precisely because of having these splotches. Without these little black spots, a work won't be considered authentically his."

A saint's life brims with the marks of sanctity and a great man's life is full of stellar accomplishments. But an ordinary life is like the pictures done by my friend: throughout, up and down, over and across, are marvelous brush strokes and wondrous black ink, while at the same time there are little, inexplicable, thick and thin black spots.

Just as sun spots are part of the sun, so too are black spots accepted as part of a picture. And now, I will tell a little of the

暈散在素面畫紙上的墨點吧！

事情是這樣的，我的身分證掉了，我自己並不知道。直到有一天我去辦公室影印一份唐詩資料才警覺。那資料是一首短歌謠，只佔半頁。我環保成性，總認為剩下半頁太可惜（雖然用的是舊紙的反面），便打算找出身分證來湊合著印，反正，身分證影本是個不時需要的文件。

但是，糟糕，它竟然不在我的皮包裡，我匆匆印完資料，把自己從全唐詩的巨帙裡拉回現實，並且追想我最後一次看到身分證是在什麼時候？啊，身分證真是一件詭異的事物——我是我，我確確實實的活著，然而一旦沒有那張巴掌大的小東西來證明我是我，我就會忽然變得什麼都不是。一百六十公分的一個人沒人承認，人家只承認六公分乘以九公分的那張小紙片。

black spots spread out on the white paper of my pedestrian life.

What had happened was this: I lost my ID card without being aware of it. I only discovered it was missing when one day I had gone to the office to photocopy some material about Tang Dynasty poetry. It was only a short folk song that just took half the sheet. A good environmentalist, I thought it was a pity to waste the other half of the sheet (even though I was using the back of already used paper) and so planned to make a copy of my ID card, a copy of which is anyway often useful.

But, much to my chagrin, it evidently was not in my purse. I hurriedly finished copying the material and, leaving the world of the classic *Complete Tang Poetry*, pulled myself back to reality. I tried to think back to the last time I had seen my ID. Oh my! What an amazing thing an ID is. I know who I am. I am certainly very much alive. But when once I no longer have that little thing no larger than the palm of my hand to prove who I am, I then suddenly turn into being no one, a person one hundred and sixty centimeters tall that no one can recognize. People will only recognize that little six cm by nine cm card.

唉，我的那張小紙片在那裡呢？我把資料丟在一旁，苦思冥想起來，一時大有「不了此事，誓不為人」的氣概。想著想著，倒也被我想起一些端倪來了，上一次，好像是去電視台；上楊照的節目，事後得了一筆錢，他們曾跟我要身分證影本供報帳，我便去印了給他們。

然而，那一次，我是在那裡影印的呢？會不會影印完了我就把它放在影印機裡忘了拿走了？想到這裡不禁悲從衷來，覺得在此茫茫五百萬人口的大城裡，走失了一個「我」。也不知這個「我」流落何方？為何人所撿拾？悲傷啊！我怎麼都不知道「我」已成為失蹤人口？

我似乎是在統一超商影印的，家附近這種店有好幾家。趁著一個不用上班的星期天，我掛著一副悲戚

Dear me! Where is that little card of mine? I tossed to one side my Tang material and started to think. Soon I had the very real determination to "resolve the predicament or just quit". I thought and I thought and I finally thought of a clue as to what might have happened. I think it was the time when I went to a television studio to be on a program of the writer and TV host Yang Chao. After it was all over I was to be paid. They wanted from me a copy of my ID card as part of the transaction and I had gone off to make a copy for them.

Now where was it that I had gone to make the copy? Could I have possibly left my ID at the photocopying machine after I had made the copy? As I thought of this, I was overcome by a certain sadness, feeling that in the midst of this vast city of five million people my "I" had disappeared, And I did not know where "I" had slipped away to. Who could have picked it up? How sad it is! How is that "I" have become a missing person.

It seems that I must have done the photocopying at a Sever-Eleven, but there are a number of such stores near my home. I took

的面容去一一走訪，彷彿去尋找「失蹤老人」或「失蹤小孩」，我殷殷打聽：

「請問有沒有人在影印機裡撿到一張身分證？」

咦？原來還真有，好心的店員拿給我看，有身分證，也有駕照，然而那一把證件上的人都不是我。我瞪著照片上那一雙雙的眼睛默默致意，希望它早日給認領回去。我繼續一家家去找，終於絕了望，嗒然返家。

彷彿是一場「自我追尋」的心理遊戲，卻碰了壁。我找不到「我」了，「我」消失了。更可怕的是，「我」可能淪落了。

這才開始悲傷起來，聽說有人專盜人家身分證去冒用，我的不必盜，只消撿就可以了。被冒用的身

advantage of a Sunday when I did not have to go to work and, with saddened face, went to visit each of these near-by stores. It was like looking for a missing elderly person or a missing child. I earnestly inquired: "Has anyone found an ID card left at the photocopying machine?"

Well, there were indeed various things. The well-intentioned clerk brought them out for me to see: ID cards and driver licenses. None of the photos, however, was mine. I stared at the pair after pair of eyes in the photos and offered my silent respect, hoping that soon someone would come, recognize them, and take the documents away. Then I continued on, going from store to store. At last I lost all hope of finding it and went home very dejected.

It was all like a psychological game of trying to "find one-self," but I had run into a dead end. My "I" was nowhere to be found, my "I" was lost. And even more frightening, my "I" was beyond retrieval.

So I became very disheartened. I heard that some people specialize in stealing ID cards for fraudulent use; but there was no

分證會變成什麼下場呢？聽說有的會賣給非法入境的人，而非法入境的女人會和色情業掛鉤，於是會有一個「我」出現在風月場中，這種事想像起來已令人魂飛魄散！又聽說有人會拿這種身分證去登記公司，於是「我」就成了董事長，人家就利用「我」去騙財，不久，「我」就有了上億的債務！啊，那張出走的「我」是可能給人家逼著去幹出各種事來的啊！「我」可以是任何人家派定的角色！

第二天是星期一，我下定決心去戶政事務所跑一趟，萬事之急，莫如此事之急。總算我還有一張戶籍謄本，一枚印章，和三張照片來作為輔佐證據，證明我自己的確是一具活著的合法生物。

我估量一下時間，電話中他們雖保證只消半小時

need to steal mine, one had only to pick it up and that would be enough. What would become of an ID that was used fraudulently? Some I had heard would be sold to those wanting to enter Taiwan illegally, some of whom would be women involved in prostitution. And so my "I" would end up at some place of sexual commerce. How terrifying it all was as I imagined what could happen! I had also heard that a stolen ID could be used to register a company. And so my "I" would become the Chairman of the Board. My "I" would be used to embezzle others out of money. Before long my "I" would be millions and millions of dollars in debt! Oh, dear me! How many of those kings of things my gone-away "I" could be forced to do. My "I" could be sent to play whatever role anyone wanted it to perform.

The next day was Monday and I decided to run over to the Bureau of Registration, knowing that nothing was more of an emergency than this. There would be a record of my registration there. My chop and three photographs could be accepted as supporting evidence that I was really a living and legal entity.

I was estimating the amount of time it would take. Even

就會辦好補發手續，但加上來去的車程，少說也要花掉一個半小時。而一個半小時是生命中多麼不可彌補的損失啊！這一個半小時如果拿來對月、當花、與朋友聊電話、為自己煮一餐端端整整的海鮮義大利麵，對著公園裡一隻小鳥發痴發楞都不算浪費，唯獨拿去辦人間繁瑣無聊的手續才真是冤哉枉也！

我一面換衣服一面恨自己，恨自己糊塗大意，因此必須付上一個半小時的「生命耗損」以為懲罰——要知道，這一個半小時是永世永劫都扳不回來的啊！我感到像守財奴掉了金子一般揪心扒肝的痛。

衣服是一套去年在廣西陽朔外貿街買的水洗絲休閒服。外貿街，是我取的名字，其實是條老街，但

though they had assured me on the phone that it would only take half an hour for the process to get a replacement, by the time travel to and from would be added on, it would take at least an hour and a half for everything, a stretch of time that if lost could never be replaced! Now it would not be considered a waste if this hour and a half could be used to enjoy the moon or smell the flowers, or to talk on the phone with a friend, or to prepare a meal of seafood spaghetti, or to daydream with the birds in the park. What would really be a disaster would be to spend this time on some mundane, complicated procedure to apply for something.

While changing my clothes, I was hating myself for being such a dolt as to cause myself to be punished by having to sacrifice an hour and a half of my life. You know very well that this hour and a half from the eons of eternity can never be retrieved. My pain was like that of a miser suffering the pain of having lost the gold which he had held on to so tightly.

The clothes I put on were a recreational outfit made of viscose that I had bought in Yangshuo, Kuanghsi Province, at the "International Trade" street. The name of the street was my own

專做老外生意。這件衣服介於藍綠色之間，鬱鬱的，像陰天的海水。衣服的質地極其柔軟，觸手柔滑如液體，我的心情稍稍好了一點。當下決定辦完手續便去朋友推薦的一家咖啡店，享受一杯咖啡，外加一塊玫瑰蛋糕。他在詩作裡曾經提過「玫瑰餅」害我垂涎，事後他坦白對我說，其實是玫瑰蛋糕，但因為湊韻律，所以改成「玫瑰餅」。詩人也真有點可惡，為了押韻竟竄改事實，散文家就比較老實。

但是，且慢，如果去喝咖啡，豈不浪費的時間更多了嗎？不，對我而言喝咖啡不叫浪費時間。生活裡的許多事都像音樂上的板眼，一個小節接著一個小節，一個二分音符等於二個四分音符，一切都得照節奏來，徐疾不得有誤。但喝咖啡的時間等於是那個延

invention. It was actually a very old street, one that spoclalized in things for trade with foreigners. The color of my outfit was somewhere between blue and green. It was on the dreary side, like the color of the sea on a cloudy day. The texture of the material was extremely soft, having a liquid suppleness. I started to feel just a little bit better and decided to stop in at a coffee shop recommended by a friend once I had applied for my new ID. There I would enjoy a cup of coffee, as well as a piece of rose cake. My friend had once, in one of his poems, referred to "rose pancakes," the mention of which made my mouth water. Afterwards he had bluntly explained to me that originally he had wanted to say "rose cake," but for the sake of the poem's rime he had changed it to "rose pancake." There's something detestable about poets that they would change a fact for the sake of rime. We essayists are a little more honest.

But, wait a moment. If I go to the coffee shop, wouldn't that mean wasting even more time? No, not at all. For me, going to a coffee shop is not a waste of time. Many things in life are like the tempo in music which goes one bar after another. One half note is equal to two quarter notes. Everything must go according to the rhythm; there can be no mistake in *andante and lente*. The

長符號，而延長符號是不納入節拍的，你愛拉多長便拉多長，它是時間方面的「外國租界」地，不歸本土管轄。它又像打籃球時叫一聲「暫停」，於是那段時間便不計在分秒必爭的戰局裡。

然而，荒謬的事發生了！就在此刻，正在我要離家去辦身分證補發申請，卻忽然覺得夾克的內層口袋裡有個怪怪的硬卡，伸手一摸，天哪，竟是我那「眾裡尋它千百度」的身分證，我以為自己永世再也見不到「我」。證上的舊日照片與我互視良久，我把它重新放入皮包。喜悅興奮當中也不免微微失望，因為不必出門了，那杯咖啡也就取消了。

這天早上我感覺恍若撿到了一張身分證，而既然有了這張身分證，我便可以冒用上面的資料好好活下

time spent drinking coffee is equal to an extended note and is outside the overall rhythm. You can extend it for as long as you want. In terms of time, it is a "foreign concession," not under the jurisdiction of the local government. Or, it is like a "time-out" during a basketball game, moments that are not counted as part of the competitive battle.

And then the preposterous event occurred. At the very moment when I was to leave home to apply for a replacement for my ID card, I suddenly realized that there was a strange, plastic card in the inner pocket of my jacket. Putting my hand in my pocket—my God—I knew it was my ID, which, as in the Sung Dynasty poem, I had been searching and searching for throughout the wide, wide world. I had thought that I would never in a hundred years see my "I" again. I looked at that old picture of me on my ID for some time and then put my ID in my purse. Nonetheless, there was just a little bit of disappointment in my excited happiness since I would now not have to go out and that cup of coffee must be canceled.

That morning I felt as if I had found an ID and that now that I had one, I could fraudulently use the information on the card and

去！我好像又有理由來憑恃而可以在這個城市裡立足了。我撿到了一個「我」——在我以為我們彼此已失之交臂的剎那。重逢不易，自宜珍惜。

這場前因後果說來真有點荒謬，不過，我不是已經說過了嗎？事情如果不帶三分荒謬，就不足以言人生。

好，我這樣告訴自己：我撿到了一張身分證，在我夾克的內層口袋裡。仔細勘驗一下，這身分證上的女子其實蠻不錯哩！

她有個很令人怦然心動的職業，她是個文學教師，她可以憑著告訴別人何以「庭院深深深幾許」是個美麗的句子而謀得衣食。讓我且來冒充她，好好登壇說法，好讓頑石也點頭。

go on with a very nice life! Now, it seemed, it was reasonable for me to take this card to be the basis to set myself up in this city. I had found my "I" at the very moment when I had thought we had lost the chance ever to see each other again. It had not been easy for us to meet again so I should cherish the occasion.

The cause and effect of all of this was a little preposterous, but hadn't I already said this: "If there's not a tinge of preposterousness to something it's really not worthwhile to be considered human."

And so this is what I said to myself: I have found an ID in the inner pocket of my jacket. As I studied it carefully, I saw that the woman on it is really quite a wonderful person!

She has a profession that could cause the heart of others to throb. She is a teacher of literature and on account of this could make a living telling others why the line of the poet Ou-yang Hsin is very beautiful ! "How deep are the unfathomably deep family grounds." So let me pretend to be her and stand on the podium and cause "stubborn stones to be enlightened."

她且有個不錯的男子為丈夫，讓我也來扮演她，跟這個男子結緣相處。

還有，她的住址也令我羨慕，我打算頂她的名，替她住在那棟能遮風避雨的好屋子裡，並且親自澆灌她養大的蘭花和馬拉巴栗樹。

啊！容許我來認真的做一做她吧！

——原載一九九八年五月十二日《聯合報》

收入九歌版《星星都已經到齊了》（2003年）

She has a wonderful man as her husband, so let me pretend to be her spending my days together with him.

And I envy her address. I plan to take her name and to take her place in her very safe and secure house. And I will personally water the orchids and American peanut trees she had cultivated.

Yes, indeed! Please allow me with all earnestness to go and be her!

"The Chinese PEN" **Winter, 1998**

月，闕也

The Moon, The Imperfect

胡守芳／譯

Translated by Shou-Fang HU-MOORE

天地是有缺陷的，但缺陷造成了縐褶，縐褶造成了奇峰幽谷之美。月亮是不能常圓的，人生不如意事十常八九；當我們心平氣和地承認這一切缺陷的時候，我們忽然發覺沒有什麼是不可以接受的。

「月，闕也」那是一本二千年前的文字專書的解釋。闕，就是「缺」的意思。

那解釋使我著迷。

曾國藩把自己的住所題作「求闕齋」，求缺。為什麼？為什麼不求完美？

那齋名也使我著迷。

「闕」有什麼好呢？「闕」簡直有點像古中國性格中的一部分，我漸漸愛上了「闕」的境界。

我不再愛花好月圓了嗎？不是的，我只是開始了解花開是一種偶然，但我同時學會了愛它們月不圓花不開的「常態」。

"The moon, the imperfect," was an interpretation written in a literary treatise about two thousand years ago. Imperfect implies "defective."

That interpretation fascinates me.

Tseng Kuo-fan[1] named his residence "Seeking Imperfection." To seek defects? Why? Why not seeking perfection?

The name of his residence also fascinates me.

What is so good about "imperfection"? "Imperfection" is almost like a part of the disposition of ancient China and I have gradually become attracted to the realms of imperfection.

Is it because I no longer love the blooming flowers and the full moon? No. I have simply begun to understand that the blooming flowers are an accidental occurrence, while also learn to appreciate "normal situations" when the moon is not full and the flowers are not blooming.

1.———Tseng Kuo-fan *(1811-1872), a high-rank official in Qing Dynasty, who was not only good at both civil and military affairs, but was also known for his academic achievements.*

在中國的傳統裡，「天殘地缺」或「天聾地啞」
的說法幾乎是毫無疑問地為一般人所接受。也許由於
長期的患難困頓，中國神話中對天地的解釋常是令人
驚訝的。

在《淮南子》裡，我們發現中國的天空和中國的
大地都是曾經受傷的。女媧以其柔和的慈手補綴撫平
了一切殘破。當時，天穿了，女媧煉五色石補了天。
地搖了，女媧折斷了神鼇的腳爪墊穩了四極（多像老
祖母疊起報紙墊桌子腿）。她又像一個能幹的主婦，
掃了一堆蘆灰，止住了洪水。

中國人一直相信天地也有其殘缺。

我非常喜歡中國西南部麼些族的神話，他們說，
天地是男神女神合造的。當時男神負責造天，女神負

In Chinese tradition, the concept of "defective heaven and earth" or "insensible heaven and earth" has been accepted by most people without any question. Maybe due to the long-standing tribulations and adversities experienced by the people, the portrayals of Heaven and Earth in Chinese mythology are often quite amazing.

From the book *Huai Nan Tzu*,[2] we discover that both the sky and earth of China have been damaged before. The Goddess Nu-wa, using her gentle hands, mended and ironed out all the fragments. At a time when the sky was broken, she melted five-colored stones to mend it. When the earth was shaken, she snapped off the feet of the legendary Turtle to stabilize its four corners—in very much the same way as our old granny would pile up newspapers to support the legs of a table. She also swept up a pile of dried reeds, like a competent housewife, to stop the flood.

Chinese people have always believed that Heaven and Earth are also not without defects.

I very much enjoy the mythology of Moso Tribe in Southwestern China. According to them, the sky and the earth

---

2.———*A collection of Chinese mythology and philosophy by Liu An, King of Huai Nan of the Han Dynasty.*

責造地。等他們各自分頭完成了天地而打算合在一起時候，可怕的事發生了；女神太勤快，她們把地造得太大了，以至於跟天沒辦法合得起來了。但是，他們終於想到了一個好辦法，他們把地折疊了起來，形成高山低谷，然後，天地才虛合起來了。

是不是西南的崇山峻嶺給他們靈感，使他們想起這則神話呢？

天地是有缺陷的，但缺陷造成了縐褶，縐褶造成了奇峰幽谷之美。月亮是不能常圓的，人生不如意事十常八九；當我們心平氣和地承認這一切缺陷的時候，便忽然發覺沒有什麼是不可以接受的。

在另一則漢民族的神話裡，說到大地曾被共工氏撞不周山時撞歪了──從此「地陷東南」，長江黃河

were created jointly by male and female gods. The male gods were responsible for making the sky and the female gods the earth. Just as they had separately finished their tasks and were ready to join them together, something terrible happened—the female gods were so over-zealous in their work that they had made the earth too big to meet the sky. However, they eventually found a way to deal with it. By folding the earth into mountains and valleys, they finally were able to join the sky and earth.

Did the sublime mountain ridges of Southwestern China inspire such a legend?

Neither the sky nor the earth is without defects, but these defects give rise to folds, and the folds bring about the beauty of majestic mountains and deep valleys. The moon cannot be full all the time, just as the course of life often goes against one's wishes. When we acknowledge all these imperfections with a peaceful mind, we suddenly realize that there is nothing intolerable in life.

Another legend of the Han people tells us that the earth was knocked lopsided when Kong-kong, the superintendent of works

便一路浩浩淼淼地向東流去，流出幾千里地驚心動魄的風景。而天空也在當時被一起撞歪了，不過歪的方向相反，是歪向西北，據說日月星辰因此嘩啦一聲大部分都倒往那個方向去了。如果某個夏夜我們抬頭而看，忽然發現群星灼灼然的方向，就讓我們相信，屬於中國的天空是「天傾西北」的吧！

五千年來，漢民族便在這歪倒傾斜的天地之間挺直脊骨生活下去，只因我們相信殘缺不但是可以接受的，而且是美麗的。

而月亮，到底曾經真正圓過嗎？

人生世上其實也沒有看過真正圓的東西。一張蔥油餅不夠圓，一塊鎳幣也不夠圓。即使是圓規畫的圓，如果用高度顯微鏡來看也不可能圓得很完美。

under Emperor Yao, was ramming Pu Chou Mountain. From then on, the earth sloped southeastwards. With it, the Yangtze River and the Yellow River in all their immensity flowed unceasingly towards the east, creating thousands of miles of soul-stirring landscape. At the same time, the sky was also thrust, though in the opposite direction, to the northwest. It was said therefore that the sun, the moon, and most of the stars all slumped towards that direction after the crash. If one summer night we look up towards the sky and find stars twinkling in that direction, we may awaken the belief within us that the sky over China does lean towards the northwest.

For more than five thousand years, the Han people have been living between the leaning sky and sloping earth with their backs straightened, simply because we believe that the imperfections are not only acceptable but also beautiful.

As for the moon, has she ever at any time been perfectly round?

In fact, there is nothing perfectly round in this universe. A pancake is not round enough, neither is a coin. Even a circle drawn with a pair of compasses, viewed under a high-powered microscope, is unlikely to be perfectly round.

真正的圓存在於理念之中，而在現實的世界裡，我們只能做圓的「複製品」。就現實的操作而言，一截圓規上的鉛筆心在畫圓的起點和終點時，已經粗細不一樣了。

所有的天體遠看都呈現球形，但並不是絕對的圓，地球是約略近於橢圓形。

就算我們承認月亮約略的圓光也算圓，它也是「方其圓時，即其缺時」。有如十二點正的鐘聲。當你聽到鐘響時，已經不是十二點了。

此外，我們更可以換個角度看。我們說月圓月闕其實是受我們有限的視覺所欺騙。有盈虛變化的是月光，而不是月球本身。月何嘗圓，又何嘗缺，它只不過像地球一樣不增不減的兀自圓著──以它那不十分圓的圓。

A perfect circle exists as a concept. But in the real world, we can only produce replicas of a circle. To carry out the task in reality, the thickness of a pencil lead in the compasses would have varied from the starting point to the end point of a circle.

All the celestial bodies look like globes from a distance, but they are not absolutely round and the earth is only approximately an oval shape.

Even if we accept the approximate roundness of a full moon as nearly exact, the reality is that no sooner has the moon become full than it also begins to wane. It is the same as the clock striking twelve. The instant when you hear the bell ringing, it is no longer twelve.

Furthermore, we can take another viewpoint. We may say that the waxing and waning of the moon is actually a deception of our limited vision. It is the moonlight, not the globe itself that changes. The moon does not wax or wane. It simply remains round — albeit with imperfect roundness — like the earth, without ever increasing or decreasing in size.

花朝月夕，固然是好的，只是真正的看花人那一刻不能賞花？在初生的綠芽嫩嫩怯怯的探頭出土時，花已暗藏在那裡。當柔軟的枝條試探地在大氣中舒手舒腳時，花隱在那裡。當蓓蕾悄然結胎時，花在那裡。當花瓣怒張時，花在那裡。當香銷紅黯委地成泥的時候，花仍在那裡，當一場雨後只見紅稀綠遍的時候，花還在那裡。當果實成熟時，花恆在那裡，甚至當果核深埋地下時，花依然在那裡⋯⋯

或見或不見，花總在那裡。或盈或缺，月總在那裡。不要做一朝的看花人吧！不要做一夕的賞月人吧！人生在世那一刻不美好完滿？那一剎不該頂禮膜拜感激歡欣呢？

因為我們愛過圓月，讓我們也愛缺月吧——它們原是同一個月亮啊！

——收入九歌版《再生緣》（2010年）

不朽的失眠｜張曉風散文中英對照
Immortal Sleeplessness

Although the morning flowers and evening moonlight are wonderful, wouldn't a real flower lover appreciate them at any other times? When the new sprouts first poke timidly through the ground, when soft branches start to stretch their limbs in the air, the flowers are already hiding within. When the buds are secretly formed or when they are in full bloom, the flowers are present. When the petals wither and fall, becoming part of the muddy ground, when the plants are covered with green leaves after a rain shower, the flowers are still there. When the fruit becomes mature or even when the seeds of the fruit have been buried deep in the ground, the flowers are there forever...

Whether one can see them or not, the flowers are always there. Whether it waxes or wanes, the moon is always there. Don't be a flower lover for one morning only. Don't simply watch the moon in one odd evening. Which moment in our life is not perfect? Which moment shouldn't we count our blessings and be thankful?

Because we have loved the full moon, let us also love her waning phases. After all, they are exactly the same moon.

"The Chinese PEN" **Winter, 2001**

十月的陽光
October Sun

施鐵民／譯　施堂模／審訂

Translated by David Steelman　Revised by Tom Sellari

　　那些氣球都飄走了，總有好幾百個罷？在透明的藍空裡浮泛著成堆的彩色，人們全都歡呼起來，彷彿自己也分沾了那份平步青雲的幸運——事情總是這樣的，輕的東西總能飄得高一點，而悲哀拽住我，有重量的物體總是注定要下沉的。

那些氣球都飄走了，總有好幾百個罷？
在透明的藍空裡浮泛著成堆的彩色，

人們全都歡呼起來，彷彿自己也分沾了那份平步青雲的幸運──事情總是這樣的，輕的東西總能飄得高一點，而悲哀拽住我，有重量的物體總是注定要下沉的。

體育場很燦爛，閃耀著晚秋的陽光，禮炮沉沉地響著，這是十月，一九六六年的十月，武昌的故事遠了。西風裡悲壯的往事遠了。

參觀證佩在胸上，人坐在看臺上，忽然不明白自己被請來，是看一齣喜劇，還是悲劇。他們在陽光下看那些發亮的頭盔，看那些褐色的胸膛，而晚上呢？還是到成都路去了，那裡有漆著黑圈的媚眼，有最現代的A-go-go。而戰爭呢？戰爭只在那些流汗的臉上，戰爭只在遙遠的岩石島上。

Balloons, hundreds of them, float up into the translucent blue sky forming shimmering masses of color.

Cheers rise up from the crowd as if the onlookers themselves were ascending to the clouds. It's always like this: light things float up so high, but heavy things always sink, and sadness drags me down.

The gun salute booms deeply through the late autumn sunlight shining down on the athletic field. On this October day[1] of 1966, the heroism of the Wuchang Revolution[2] seems so distant.

Observers sit in the stands, visitor's badges on their chests. I suddenly begin to wonder whether I have been invited to witness a commemoration of glory or tragedy. They're looking at the helmets glinting under the sun and the deeply tanned chests. And in the evening? They will go downtown where there are women with painted eyes and go-go dancers. And the war? The war is on the faces of the soldiers sweating in the sun. The war is on the rocky islands of Kinmen.[3]

1.———*October 10, or Double Tenth, is the anniversary of the founding of the Republic of China.*

2.———*The revolution in 1911 which overthrew the Ching Dynasty and established the Republic.*

3.———*Also known as Quemoy, an island complex at the mouth of Amoy bay about 160 nautical miles from Taiwan, is the frontline redoubt of the Republic of China. The*

那些人全立在揚起的灰塵裡，在我們的背後，聖火燃燒著，聽說那是從金門太武山傳來的火種（又聽說那是一個很遙遠的地方，和我們成都路的距離須要用光年計算），當那位少校英雄持著火把去點燃那一炷聖火的時候，看臺上全是掌聲，從肥厚多肉的手掌中拍出來，也從柔若無骨的纖手中拍出來，然後他們坐下，很小心的坐在鋪了手帕或報紙的看臺上。

而那些人卻立在灰塵裡，他們年輕的臉被灰塵隔得模糊而不真實。忽然那些人影退得很遠，草場上只剩下一則一則的故事，從塞北，從江南，那些相同的濡滿淚水的故事。十七年以前，十八年以前或者更早，便是那些故事的開場。那些男孩子走在田埂上，回望著庭裡的一株桃樹，淒迷的紅霧便浸濕在淚眼裡，故園從此不見了，而故事擱淺在一個多棕櫚的島上。一則則的故事，在十月的陽光裡閃躲，想閃開那些可憐的故園中的一抹微紅，想閃開孤燈下母親頭上的一莖白髮。

The soldiers stand before us in the dusty field and behind us burns a great torch. They say the fire was brought all the way from Mount Taiwu on Kinmen. (They say that it's a far-away place, so distant from our neon signs and night clubs that the distance has to be measured in light-years.) A major carries the fire up to light the torch, and the stands are filled with applause, fat meaty hands striking fat meaty hands, slender delicate hands patting slender delicate hands. Then they all sit down carefully on handkerchiefs and newspapers spread out on the stands.

The soldiers are lined up on the field, their youthful faces blurred by the dust, which makes them seem unreal. Suddenly they seem to fade into the distance, leaving on the field only ghosts of long past wars,[4] ghosts of boys walking along the narrow paths of the rice paddies, looking back at the peach tree in the courtyard for the last time as their tears mixed with the sun-streaked mists. Haunting memories of seventeen, eighteen, and more years ago flit through the October sun: a red splotched sky over the old home... a solitary light bulb illuminating the white hair of the woman seated underneath, memories stranded on an island of palm trees.

Chinese Communists have made several futile attempts to invade Kinmen, most notable of which was the artillery barrage starting on Aug. 23, 1958 in which the Communists hurled half a million shells at the island in 44 days.

4.———*Wars against the Chinese Communists.*

　　紅色大柱子下坐著文武百官，那柱子仍然保留著
一些東方的自尊，一些恢弘的氣象，這幾乎有點像太
平盛世了。從小小的觀劇鏡裡望出去，那八十歲的統
帥正坐在中央，那張不曾老去的臉依然刻劃著黃埔，
依然刻劃著廣州誓師，那樣抿著的嘴和沉思的眼睛牽
動著一個時代的命運，而他坐在這裡，他的心中翻騰
著些什麼呢？半個世紀過去了，離亂的中國人民苦痛
著，中國人並不吉卜賽，我們是一種即使死在火星上
也要把骸骨搬回來的民族。天知道當我們放棄田園而
浪跡天涯的時候是一齣怎樣的悲劇。

　　只是有一些人已經不悲劇了，他們很滿意地說，
現在的雲南大頭菜挺不錯，金華火腿也算差強人意
了，而水蜜桃兒不是也很像那麼回事嗎？當他們坐在
筵席上的時候，喝的是浙江的紹興酒，手裡握著的是
湖南的長筷子，端上來的菜卻有鎮江的肴肉，廣東的
白斬雞，北平的烤鴨，四川的辣子雞丁，他們舔舔嘴
唇說：這裡很好。

The government and military leaders are seated in a pavilion under ornately decorated red pillars which preserve a vestige of the dignity and splendor of the Orient. For a moment it almost seems as if peace has descended on earth. The eighty-year-old leader[5] can be seen seated in the center. His long military career is etched on his face. The fate of an age has been determined by those solemn lips and pensive eyes. What is he thinking as he sits there? Half a century has gone by. Scattered by war, the Chinese people suffer. The Chinese are not gypsies. Even if we died on Mars our bones would have to be returned to their proper resting place. Only heaven knows the tragedy set in motion as we abandoned our homes and began wandering.

But for some, the tragedy is already over. They feel very satisfied. The Yunnan-style preserved mustard root isn't too bad. The Chinhua-style ham is passable and the peaches are just about as good. When they sit at their banquets, they drink Shaohsingrice wine and eat with long chopsticks as in Hunan. They eat dishes like Chinkiang pork, Cantonese white sliced chicken, Peiping roast duck, Szechuan spicy diced chicken. They lick their lips and say, "It's all right here."

5.——President Chiang Kai-shek, 1888-1975, who led the Northern Expedition against warlords in 1926-28, the Sino-Japanese war in 1937-45, and the war against the Chinese Communists.

真的。很好，什麼都有了——除了秋日該有歸思以外，我們是什麼都有了。

他坐在那裡，那八十歲的三軍統帥，他的心裡翻騰著復國！他是不願再坐在這裡了，我知道的。六千多個在淚裡沉浮的日子，我們過夠了，中山陵上的落葉已深，我們的手臂因渴望一個掃墓的動作而痠痛。

那些節目進行著，美麗的白刃在陽光裡閃著淒冷的光圈，它們等待喝血的日子已經等足了一個世紀了，而敵人那樣遙遠，我們的刺刀因貧血而蒼白，長長的血槽十七年來除了擦槍油再沒有別的飲料。

對了，飲料，聽說蘋果西打的銷路已經超過黑松，而榮冠可樂又取代了蘋果西打。哈，原來我們也進步得跟喝可口可樂的民族一樣文明了，好漂亮的鴆汁，分六種不同的口味（六塊錢一瓶，岩石島上浴血者的一日所得），我們坦然地喝著，用一根細細的麥

Yes, it's fine. We're got everything here, everything but the thoughts of returning home, which should come with autumn.

He sits there, the eighty-year-old leader, with thoughts of returning to the mainland running through his mind. He doesn't want to sit here, I know. More than six thousand days of bobbing up and down in an ocean of tears, we've already had enough. Our hands ache with the longing to sweep the deep layers of leaves covering Sun Yat-sen's tomb.[6]

The review continues. The white bayonets glint coldly in the sun. How long they have waited to drink blood, and yet the enemy is so far away. Our bayonets are pale and anemic. For the past seventeen years they haven't had anything to drink but gun oil.

Drinks, yes... They say Apple Cider is selling better than Hei Sung soda, and Royal Crown sales have surpassed Apple Cider. Ha, so we've achieved the same degree of civilization that the Coca Cola drinkers have. What beautiful liquids in six different flavors, (six dollars a bottle, the same as a day's pay for the front line soldiers on Kinmen). Through thin wheat-straws we drink without a second

---

6.———*Dr. Sun Yat-sen is the founding father of the Republic of China. His tomb is in Nanking, the capital of the Republic of China.*

管，喝那加了透明冰塊的一日所得。然後我們看報紙，看那些很遙遠的戰爭，在越南的或者在剛果的，然後我們睡覺，養足精神去看今晚觀光飯店裡的脫衣舞。

當單純的鼓聲響起的時候，那些蛙人便戴著潛水鏡出場了。他們全都那樣年輕，有著同色調的紫褐色的肉。多麼漂亮的男人，在陽光下的只著一條短褲的漂亮男人，真是能教女人發抖的，而他們的動作亮在原始的鼓聲裡，有著可愛的粗野。

其實，說起來很多人都不信的，我們已經很久沒有見過男人了。在我們的城市裡，充斥的只是那種穿西裝、打領帶的生物，那種既沒有骨骼也沒有血液的生物，那種偷偷地在枕頭下面藏著「海狗丸」的生物。

而這裡有很多男人，強壯得令女人發抖的男人，他們卻是沒有女人的。他們在水裡在沙裡的時間也許比陸地上的多，陸地上的溫柔他們是沒有份的，海

thought one day's pay with transparent ice-cubes. We pick up the newspaper and read about far-off wars in Vietnam and the Congo and then take a nap so we'll be fresh for the nightclub acts.

Drums sound and the frogmen march onto the field wearing their masks. Clad only in shorts, they move under the sun... such young, bronze-skinned, beautiful bodies that send tingles up a woman's spine, so masculine as they move to the primitive beat of drums.

People wouldn't believe it but we haven't seen any "men" for a long time. Our cities are filled with bloodless, spineless creatures wearing suits and ties who secretly keep a bottle of "Seal Pills"[7] under their pillows.

But here there are lots of men, strong men who make a woman tremble. But they have no women. They spend more time in the water and on beaches than they do on land. They have no share in

---

7.———A restorative for men.

水、天風環逼著他們，他們的世界裡沒有麻將，沒有酒和酒後的溫柔，他們只有殺人，或者被人殺。

想起殺人，想起海灘上和海底下的肉搏，秋意就忽然濃起來了。那些可愛的男人，他們有時也會被殺的，那真是不能想像。可是，事實上，他們中間許多人出海以後便沒有再回來了，那樣漂亮得令人發抖的肌肉！

看臺上有輕輕的驚呼，驚奇那些灰塵中的人能演出那樣的動作，他們說：「啊！天哪！」他們笑（很溫雅的），又搖頭，互相讚歎。我忽然覺得冷意從齒齦間升起，憤怒使我全身發抖── 我拚命把雙腳踏穩，但總覺得整個看臺都被我弄得抖了起來，他們竟敢那樣不在乎的鼓掌，他們竟敢面對赴湯蹈火的壯士而不動容。他們算什麼？他們憑什麼？他們為什麼能笑，我敢說，除了股票跌價的那陣子，他們是沒有哭過的。

the land's sweetness. They are driven by the oceans and winds in a world without mahjong, wine, or the tenderness that comes after wine. They have only killing... and being killed.

When I think of the deaths and the hand-to-hand combat on the beaches, my feeling of desolation deepens. Those beautiful men —sometimes they are killed. It's unimaginable but true. Many of them never return from their mission in the sea, those beautiful bodies that quicken a woman's blood.

Murmers of surprise issue from the stands as the spectators watch, amazed at the movements of the frogmen. "My god!" they say, smiling gently. Heads shake as they exchange words of praise. Suddenly I feel a cold shiver well up inside me, and my whole body trembles with anger. I press my feet down firmly with all my strength but I still feel as if I have made the stands quiver. How could they applaud so unconcernedly? How dare they look at these heros of war with such indifference? Who are they to sit in such indifference? How can they laugh? I'm sure they've never cried, except when the stock market fell.

　　雜在他們中間有許多外國人，很有興味地坐在那裡看這些「落後民族」能演出什麼把戲。那些金髮、銀髮和棕髮的女人都戴著好看的帽子，好看得令人嫉妒，她們是死也不會忘記她們美麗昂貴的帽子的——而我們是沒有帽子的民族，頂在我們黑髮上的除了炎黃子孫那份無可奈何的驕傲就再沒有別的了。

　　而他們的男人拿著望遠鏡，優閒地坐著。他們那種姿勢和他們在義大利聽歌劇，在西班牙看鬥牛並沒有兩樣——當然並不需要兩樣，戰爭對他們來說是既遙遠又陌生的事，他們只不過是花了錢到別處來表演自大的一些傢伙。我們能多要求什麼呢？沒有人有替別人死的義務，我們生氣，只不過出於嫉妒罷了。嫉妒他們有那樣太平的歲月，有那樣昌隆的國運，就像我們嫉妒那些好看的帽子一樣。

　　亮著汗水的胸膛退去了，他們背上全是泥沙，貴賓全都很滿意，外賓也都讚賞著，只差沒有人叫「安

Mixed among the spectators are a number of foreigners looking on with curiosity to see what of a show this "backward race" will put on. The blond-, silver-, and brown-haired women wear beautiful hats, beautiful enough to envy. They would never leave their fancy hats behind. And us, we're a hatless people with nothing to cover our black hair but the inherited pride of Emperor Huang Ti's[8] descendants.

Their men leisurely look through binoculars as if they were watching an opera in Italy or a bullfight in Spain. Of course there is no reason why they should act any differently. The war is distant and strange to them. They have only come to show off their complacent superiority. What more can we expect of them? No one has the obligation to die for anyone else. We are angry because we are envious, that's all. We envy their peace and national prosperity just as we envy their expensive hats.

The bodies glisten with perspiration as they move off the field, their backs covered with dirt. The spectators seem very satisfied, the

---

8.———*Emperor Huang Ti, a distinguished leader about forty-six centuries ago. It was during his reign that Chinese recorded history began.*

可」。

那些刺刀，那些汗，那些肌肉全都退去了，那些「一！二！三！四！」，那些「殺！」「嘿！」也停止了。人們把印得很古典的參觀手冊拿來搧涼，想搧走十月裡代替了薄霜的陽光，想搧走戰爭，而搧不走的是滿體育館「殺」的餘音，那蒼涼的，喊了十七年而仍未能施展的吶喊。

然後彩色煙幕輕快地劃下了十二道雲霞，全場歡呼雷動，我忽然忍不住地哭泣了，那十二道彩色在空中停留著，像一群漂亮的龍，卻怎麼也舞不出一個太平盛世的年景來，戰爭仍在，那忘不掉的海峽上的陰影。

起來吧，今天晚上第五水門有很好看的煙花，那煙花有既典雅又響亮的名字，有既輝煌又燦爛的幻

foreign guests are also full of praises. The only thing lacking is a call for an encore.

The bayonets, the sweat, the muscular bodies, have all left the field. Just the "hut, two, hut, two's," the "kill," the grunts of fighters are left floating in the still air. People pick up their engraved programs and fan themselves, to fan away the sun which chases away the October morning frost, or to fan away the war. But they cannot fan away the echoes of the battle cries that hover over the field, the cries that have been shouted for seventeen years yet are still unable to be put to actual use.

Afterwards, airplanes lace the sky with twelve streams of color and the audience cheers wildly. Suddenly, I can't help crying. The twelve streams of color pause in the air like a group of painted dragons. But their dance can't bring forth an age of peace. The war still goes on, a dark shadow over the Taiwan Straits.

Come on, get up. There is a fireworks display by the dam tonight, dozens of different kinds of fireworks, each with a different beautiful name, each bringing such a glorious fantasy that the

象，戰爭那名詞是該被忘掉的。你看，別人不是可以忘掉的嗎？你比他們年輕，你離開故園的時候只不過是一個沒有記憶的孩子，而他們忘了，你何必固執的記著呢？

看台在一霎間就空了，草場也空了，彩色煙幕變得散亂而又稀薄，我依然坐著，對著紅色的大柱子哭泣，十月的秋陽在淚光裡碎成一千個，一千個秋日的歸思。

忽然從什麼地方有淡淡的荷香飄來，浮在陽光裡，猛然警覺這正是那年秋天在玄武湖深處所發現的那朵荷花的清香，但那香味在我抬起頭來的瞬間忽然退去了，像那些彩色煙幕，變得那樣遙遠模糊。我忍不住地再度哭出聲來——我分不出我是哭那遙遠的故國的荷香，還是哭這島上廉價的陽光？

——選自道聲版《曉風散文集》（1977年）

name of war should be forgotten. Your see—everyone else can forget. You're younger than they are. You left your home before you were old enough to remember. They've forgotten. Why do you still remember stubbornly?

The stands empty rapidly, leaving the field vacant . Faint traces of the smoke trails are still scattered in the sky. But I still sit there crying to the red pillars, and my tears break the October sun into a thousand suns and a thousand autumn memories of home.

A faint fragrance of lotus flowers floats through the sunlit air. I suddenly remember this fragrance as the delicate lotus scent on the Hsuanwu lake in Nanking.[9] But the instant I lift my head it's gone, into the distance like the streams of colored smoke. I can't help crying again. But for what: for the lotus flowers far away in Nanking, or for the ever-present sunlight over this island?

"The Chinese PEN" Spring, 1975.

9.——— *The capital of the Republic of China.*

不是遊記

Not a Travelogue

吳敏嘉／譯

Translated by Michelle M. Wu

　　然後，飛機才正式著陸，一種乍然沉船的感覺。香港到了，香港是
一齣充滿丑角和笑鬧的悲劇。人世間還有何城市像這座城一樣同時擁有
狂歡的霓虹和死亡的陰影？

不能放棄的瘦疼

既沒有看見什麼依山而築的別墅，
也沒有看見什麼銜尾優游的小船。
倒是那麼巨幅的汽水廣告，在措不及防中跳進了視線，心中便突然像飲了那滿杯冒著泡子的辛辣，無端地悲哀了起來。

然後，飛機才正式著陸，一種乍然沉船的感覺。香港到了，香港是一齣充滿丑角和笑鬧的悲劇。人世間還有何城市像這座城一樣同時擁有狂歡的霓虹和死亡的陰影？

於是，才看到那一塊塊比座標紙還規則的公寓，每一戶都晾著些不十分白的衣服，在正午的懶風中待飄不飄的，猛一看，恍惚覺得是某種老屋的窗紙，又破又乾地裂成一種敗落的形象。

The Pain that I Cannot Relinquish

I did not see villas on the mountains, nor did I see picturesque little boats.
What leaped into my eye was the huge billboard advertising soda pop, and for no apparent reason, my heart started to ache as if it had just drunk up the glass full of pungent bubbles.

The plane then landed, like a sinking boat that suddenly hit bottom. I had arrived in Hong Kong. Hong Kong, a tragedy filled with clowns and farces. Is there any other city in the world that possesses such wild ecstasy and the shadow of death simultaneously?

And then, I saw the apartments, block after block as symmetrical as ruled paper. Hanging outside of almost every apartment for airing were clothes that were not very white, hanging still, waiting for the lazy breezes of noon. At first glance, they looked like the paper windows of old houses, torn and brittle, all shabbiness.

　　再然後，才在甬道裡看到「靠左走」的牌子，兩個簡單的英文字倒使我在其下呆立了許久。「反其道而行」的世界又是怎樣的世界？

　　滿街亂撲的豔陽下，偶見的樹色似乎都清新，讓人怎麼也想不起兩年前曾有怎樣令人心悸的日子。沿著左，車子開向沙田，小兒詩詩在我的臂上睡了，這城市的彩色不曾投上他的睡睫。

　　「這灣海，」許說，「就要填起來了。」

　　我抬眼望那不十分青綠的山，忍不住的悲憫便湧上來，不久後，此處將無山，山都將屈服於剷土機，成為一擔擔的泥。而水，那又淺又亮的水也將沒有了──在一片片的黃泥之下，水將被埋葬。

Later, in the underpass, I saw the sign "Keep Left." The two simple English words rendered me motionless for a long while. What kind of world is this that directs people to "move in the opposite way"?[1]

Under the bouncing rays of the sun that filled the streets, the trees that intermittently caught my eyes looked fresh and green, making it difficult for one to remember the terrifying days two years ago.[2] Driving to the left, the car moved towards Shatin and my son, Shih-shih had fallen asleep in my arms. The colors of this city have not yet been projected into his sleeping eyes.

"This bay," Hsu said, "is going to be filled up."

I looked towards the not very verdant mountains, and was overwhelmed by waves of compassion and pity that came swelling up inside me. Soon, there would be no mountains here. The mountains would surrender to the bulldozer, becoming pile after pile of dirt. And the water, the shallow and shiny water, will disappear—buried under the yellow earth.

1.——*in Hong Kong, pedestrians and traffic keep to the left, opposite to Taiwan, where pedestrians and traffic keep to the right.*

2.——*The author is referring to the mass riots that took place in Hong Kong in 1968, following the 1966 Cultural Revolution on mainland China.*

「沒有辦法，」無奈的聲音從前座傳來，「那邊
每年要跑過來五萬人。」

五萬，亂世裡一個怎樣不值錢的數目。

淺海裡的陽光異樣地刺目，我轉過臉，像避開電
影中某個悲慘的鏡頭。而垂首處，詩詩的午夢清熟，
一朵笑意自他的黑睫撒下，他沉重的頭壓著我，那重
量讓人覺得多麼像鄉愁──它壓得你痠疼，但你不能
放棄。

「你要去邊界嗎？」許說，「我去過幾次，再也
不忍去了，那種古來未有的傷心地竟讓外國人當觀光
區了。」

平穩的路上車子似乎忽然顛簸得不能忍受，滿眼
的山色一霎間便模糊了起來。

"We have no choice," Hsu's voice came from the front seat, "fifty thousand people run over from the other side every year."

Fifty thousand, a number that doesn't amount to much in this chaotic world.

The rays of the sun reflected on the shallow sea were extraordinarily prickly to the eye. I turned my head away, as if avoiding an unbearable scene in a movie. Shih-shih was fast asleep, a trace of smile spreading around his eyelashes. The weight of his head pressing heavily against me felt so much like nostalgia—it presses down on you till it hurts, but you cannot relinquish it.

"Do you want to go to the border?" Hsu asked, "I've been there several times, but now I can't bear to go anymore. The sadness of that place is unparalleled in history, yet the site has become a tourist destination for foreigners."

Suddenly, the car ride became unbearably bumpy, even though the road was smooth. The view of the mountain grew blurred in my eyes.

苦芥

　　崇基書院是一個小小的山莊，我驚訝於那重疊的綠嶂，和那些隱現的曲徑，曲徑的低處是我的小屋——那只有兩面牆的小屋。小屋的另兩面全是白漆的窗，那麼怡人地開向大片的草地和海水。

　　如果只是演講，只是對著這一帶耀眼的綠，三個禮拜又算什麼？但如果要負荷鄉愁呢？如果要同時思念那條多柳的新生南路與多煙的二十四橋呢？

　　餐廳裡，每張桌上都有一瓶塑膠花，花雖肖似，卻不見動人，倒是那瓷瓶，頗有一種景泰藍的趣味，但一看瓶底所標明的出品地，我便愣住了，瓶中的細砂石索索地撒了一桌。

Bitter Mustard

The Chung Chi College is a little villa in the mountains. I was surprised by the layers of green hills and the hidden winding paths leading to my little house. My house has two walls only. The other two sides of the house are windows with painted white frames, pleasantly opening over expanses of green fields and the sea.

If I were only here to give a speech, and have in front of me this swatch of sparkling green, why should I worry about the coming three weeks? But what if one were to bear the weight of nostalgia? And what if I were to think both of the willow-tree-lined Xinsheng South Road[3] and the misty Twenty-four Bridges[4] at the same breath?

In the dining hall, there was a vase of plastic flowers on every table. The flowers were good imitations, though not especially striking. But the ceramic vase was interesting, looking very much like cloisonné.A look at the origin under the vase, however, left me dumbfounded, making me spill the sand in the vase all over the table.[5]

3.———*A street in Taipei, where the author resides.*
4.———*A scenic spot in Yan-chou, south of the Yang-tze River, in China.*
5.——— *The vase was made in China.*

　　奇怪的是面對著二十年來唯一見到的敵人物品，心中竟泛不出一絲恨意。摸著那光豔的釉彩，心中所想的只是故土上某個窰匠枯瘦的手，只是二十年來他在死去的中國瓷上所滴下的，比釉彩還紅的淚。

　　晚餐的桌上有人說：「我們這裡什麼都沒有，我們連吃的青菜都是從那邊來的。」

　　我停箸望他，疑惑地指著在鮑魚下的苦芥說：「這也是那邊來的嗎？」

　　「是的。」

　　我黯然良久，感到方才吃下的那特別的苦味一直苦到趾尖。

　　有生之日，我知道，這悲劇的苦味將永遠被反芻。

Strangely speaking, as I was confronted with something made by the *enemy* for the first time in twenty years, I felt no hatred at all in my heart. As I touched the sparkling glaze, all I could think of was the wrinkled hand of a craftsman at a kiln somewhere on the Mainland, my forsaken homeland. The tears that he shed on this piece of china from the China that died twenty years ago, however, are redder than the glaze on the vase.

At the dinner table someone said, "We don't have anything here, even the vegetables that we eat are from the other side."

Confused, I point to the bitter mustard under the abalone, "Is this from that side too?"

"Yes."

I was grief-stricken for a long while, feeling the bitterness that I just swallowed spread all the way down to my toes.

For as long as I live, I know, I will ruminate on the bitterness of this tragedy over and over again.

碎成節的

夜裡醒來，半窗昏月，滿谷蟲鳴。一條黃昏時分明看見在幾十公尺外的山泉，此刻竟響得像在枕上流過的。

客裡的愁情到此一併而發。

草場盡處的火車碾過鋼，也碾過我不寐的雙耳。

「火車開向那裡？」白天，我曾這樣問別人。

「往這邊是九龍。」一個女孩告訴我。

「那邊呢？」

「那邊是上水和羅湖 —— 再過去就要到廣州了。」

Broken into Fragments

I woke up in the middle of the night, to a hazy moon outside the half-closed window, and a valley full of chirping insects. The mountain spring which I had judged to be dozens of meters away in the late afternoon yesterday, now sounded as if it were flowing over my pillows.

My heart burst with homesickness.

At the far end of the grassy field, the trains rolled over the steel tracks, and over my sleepless ears.

"Where does the train go ?" I had asked someone during the day.

"Kowloon, if it moves in our direction." A girl told me.

"And the other direction?

"Sheng Shui and Lo Wu—going farther, and you get to Guangzhou."

「只要換一班車就到廣州了嗎？」

「大概是的吧？」

凝視著那黑色的車廂，第一次發覺火車竟有那麼沉重，重得竟碎成那麼多節。

而此刻，在黑如深淵的夜裡，鳴笛是殘忍的閃電，裂開席夢思上的夢，裂開長簾下一個孩子均勻地，大提琴般低柔的鼾聲。

上水。羅湖。廣州。火車。碎成節的。珠江大橋。愛群酒家。多麼接近的遙遠，多麼陌生的熟稔。

火車向北，火車向南，火車永遠在輾。

"Will one transfer by train take one to Guangzhou?"

"I guess so."

Staring at the black carriages of the train, I discovered for the first time the heaviness of the train. The heaviness crushed the train into many sections.

At this moment, in the abysmally dark night, the shrill whistle of the train is a cruel streak of lightning, shattering dreams, and splitting the even, cello-like snoring of a kid sleeping under the long curtains.

Sheung Shui, Lo Wu. Guangzhou. Train. Broken into fragments. Zhujiang Bridge.[6] Aichun Restaurant.[7] So distant, yet how close by. So strange, yet how familiar.

Trains going north, trains going south, trains in perpetual grinding.

6.———*Also known as the Pearl River Bridge, in Guangdong.*

7.———*A restaurant in Guangzhou which used to be the tallest and most luxurious restaurant before China fell to the Communists in 1949.*

白　鳥

　　早晨十一時，山坡上的小松樹剛剛曬乾，可口可樂的罐子在地下滾動。我拿起一枝筆，想在名片的背面畫一幅對面的水田，筆觸未到，淚卻先至。小小的長著小松的小山坡，一口氣可以跑完的小山坡，而二十年過去，結辮的小女孩已是母親，故國的路卻仍遙遠。山河漸碎，碎如淚，筆觸未到，淚已先至。

　　深圳河，怎樣黃濁而又怎麼滯重的一條河。赤柱的海水快意地藍著，淺水灣的海水輕鬆地亮著，而世上竟有深圳，黃如墳土渾如膽汁的深圳。刺人如一條魚鯁的深圳，悲哀如一痕內傷的深圳。永生永世不能痊癒的深圳。

　　山色殘忍地青著，水牛殘忍地悠閒著，一隻白鳥

White Bird

It's eleven o'clock in the morning. The little pine trees on the hill have just been dried by the sun, and a Coca-cola[8] can rolls on the ground. I pick up a pen, wanting to draw a picture of the rice paddies before me, but suddenly burst into tears. This is a tiny little hill with little pine trees. It is so tiny that one can run around it in one breath. Twenty years have passed, and the little girl in braids is now a mother, but the road leading back to my forsaken homeland is still long and winding. The mountains and rivers of my homeland stand fragmented, as fragmented as my heart, and the tears that I have shed.

The yellow and murky Shenzhen River, what a stagnant and heavy river. The sea water of Stanley Beach is a delightful blue, and the sea water of Repulse Bay sparkles cheerfully, but there is Shenzhen, as yellow as a funeral mound, and as murky as bile. Shenzhen, as sorrowful as a smarting internal wound. A wound that will never heal.

The mountain looks cruelly green, the water buffalo walks

8.———*Coca Cola has been transliterated into ke-ko ke-le, meaning "tasty and uplifting."*

殘忍地往返於河面，分明仍是王維的山水，分明仍是
倪雲林的山水——如果沒有鐵絲網，如果沒有巡警。

日光白如飛塵，飛塵白如日光，嗆鼻的乾燥中，
只有深圳河是永不止息的淚溝。八月，飲冰的季節，
我的心卻只能飲恨，只能飲二十年流不盡的憂傷。

一座漂亮的彩色飛亭可笑地站在山頭，亭下站著
一個可笑的賣畫人，在眩耀那些廉價的油彩，面對
著僵死的山河，他何竟能畫出那樣橘紅的落日，那樣
繽紛的船影。三十元一幅，或者二十元，山河可以標
售，風景可以打折。小攤上並且有明信片，兜售著中
國人最悲涼的故事。

筆在手，畫在目，淚在兩岸臨風。風無聲，淚無

cruelly at a leisurely pace, and a white bird flies cruelly back and forth across the river. This is a perfect pastoral scene depicted in classical Chinese poetry and landscape paintings—if only there were no barbed wire and patrolling policemen to spoil the picture.

The incandescent sunlight and the equally brightly lit dust in the air make it very difficult to breath. In the choking aridity, the Shenzhen River is the only conduit flowing with tears that will never run dry. August is the season for tall icy drinks. Yet, my heart can only drink the grievance, and twenty years of endless sorrow.

A gaudy pavilion with flying cornices stands on top of the mountain, looking somewhat ludicrous. Under the pavilion stands a vendor displaying cheap oil paintings for sale. In the presence of so stagnant and dead a landscape, how and where did he get such orange sunsets and colorful boats? For thirty or twenty dollars apiece, mountains and rivers were offered for bids, and scenery sold at a discount. The vendor also sells postcards that tell the saddest stories of the Chinese people.

Pen in hand, I look down at the two sides of the river, my tears

聲，畫無聲，筆無聲。唯深圳河，響自受創的肺腑。

走下山徑，看見的可口可樂在路側堆疊，我哭了。世上有何物可適失鄉者之口，世上又復有何事可樂懷愁者之心。

白鳥在此岸，白鳥在彼岸，白鳥翩翩著古代的翅膀，水牛蹣跚著老式的悠閒，山巒摺疊著國畫的皴法。有異的是山河，不殊的是風景。

紙片的一面繪著深圳，紙片的另一面是我的籍貫和名字——薄薄的一紙是迢迢的河漢，薄薄的一紙是無鵲可渡的無限遠。

二十年，深圳。深圳，悲哀如一痕內傷的深圳。

streaming down in the wind. Everything—my pen, my tears, the wind, and the scenery, remains silent. Except for the Shenzhen River, roaring from the depths of its wounded heart and soul.

Walking down the pathway, I saw Coca Cola bottles piled on the side, and I broke into tears. What is there in this world that can satisfy the palate of one who is cut off from one's homeland? What is there in this world that can cheer up a heart so heavy with sorrow?

The white bird flies back and forth across the river, flapping its timeless wings. The water buffalo strolls at an old-fashioned leisurely pace. The mountains appear furrowed with overlapping wrinkles as seen in classical Chinese paintings. The country has changed hands, but the scenery remains constant.

On one side of the card, I have painted Shenzhen. On the other side, my name and birth place. However, the distance between the two sides of the paper is a Milky Way that no magpie can cross[9].

Twenty years, Shenzhen. The sad-as-an-internal-wound-Shenzhen.

9.———*This is an allusion to the Chinese myth "The Cow-herder and the Spinner-girl." The two lovers are separated by the Milky Way, and can only meet on the seventh day of the seventh month of the lunar calendar every year, when magpies form a bridge for them to cross over and meet each other in sweet embrace.*

彩色的遊戲

隔著海，望香港的燈火，香港不見，只見一片霓虹。城市是什麼？城市或者只是一種彩色的遊戲。曾在巴比倫玩過的，曾在羅馬玩過的，現在又在香港和九龍被玩了。下一站，歷史的下一站又是什麼？

彌敦道上，兩層的巴士飛馳。人群像千足蟲，重複著永遠走不完的腳，在人行道上匆匆來去。忽而穿行在熱流中，忽而被大公司的冷氣襲中。人們永不能了解自己是在赤道，或是南極？是在洪荒年代，或是二十世紀？

午夜三點，在朋友家中被吵醒，身在十三層樓上一個最蔽靜的房間裡，卻疑惑是被踩在暴動的人潮之下。城市，城市是什麼？是聲音的競技場嗎？

The Game of Colors

Looking across the sea, I can see Hong Kong's lights, but not the city of Hong Kong. I can only see masses of neon lights. What is a city? A city may just be a game of colors, one that was played in Babylon, in Rome, and now in Hong Kong and Kowloon. And the next stop, where is history's next stop?

On Nathan Road, double-decker buses speed by. The crowds of people are like centipedes, repeating their never-ending footsteps, rushing to and fro on the sidewalks, walking in hot, simmering air one moment and getting hit by cold drafts leaking from air-conditioned commercial buildings the next. They can never tell where they are: the equator or the South Pole? The dawn of time or the twentieth century?

I was awoken at three o'clock in the morning. There I was in the quietest room on the thirteenth floor at my friend's place, yet I wondered if I was being stampeded by a violent crowd. The city—what is a city? An arena of noise?

不寐時，便想到那天晚上的街景，皇后道上不知何處駛來張惶的救火車，怪異的燈光下，街邊的噴泉忽然變色，噴著憤怒，噴著憂鬱，噴著寞落，噴著死。而碼頭上的汽油霓虹廣告，把海水染紅又染綠，讓人想起古老的海戰，讓人想起血流飄杵的人類史。

不能忘記黃昏時，四起的燈光裡，亞皆老街上站著一個髮綹如蛇的瘋子，顛躓著步履，斜披著襤褸，被貼在一街川流的繁華上，像一個黏錯了的手工。

還有那些龍，一條條被塑在大廈門前的，此刻，在午夜三點，不知是否也疲於張牙舞爪，疲於它古老的驕傲。每次看見它，就彷彿看見沉甸甸的中國，被釘在大廈的門楣上，任過往的市聲溺死，任紛落的市塵壓死。

Suffering from insomnia, I thought of the street scenes of that night: a frantic fire truck screeching down Queen's Road, and, in the phantasmagorical lights, the fountain on the street suddenly changed colors—spurting anger, spurting sadness, spurting loneliness, spurting death, with the neon billboard on the pier coloring the sea water red and green, conjuring up ancient sea battles, reminiscent of the history of the mankind, full of blood and strife.

I cannot forget the scene at sunset. As the street lamps lit up, I saw a deranged man with Medusa-like hair and cloaked in rags, stumbling and tottering down Argyle Street—a montage incongruously set against a street pulsating with prosperity.

And the dragons, sculpted on the doorway of the building, one alongside the other. I wonder if they at three o'clock in the morning are also weary of baring their teeth and gnashing their claws, weary of their ancient pride. Every time I see the dragon, I seem to see China—weighted-down, nailed to the doorway of a big building, to be drowned by the incessant noise of the city, and crushed by the cascading city dust.

大廈樓梯間裡的白紙，在夜色裡忽然也特別地粲明起來——大廈是另一種破廟，在逃荒的年代。樓梯是床，紙是褥，希臘哲人的木桶到此也成了負荷。生活究竟可以赤裸到怎樣的程度？流亡的故事究竟可以寫成怎樣的慘淡。城不寐，我亦不寐，相對的清醒中唯彩色在周流，在永無止息地玩著漸漸疲乏的遊戲。

山

有一天，沒有太陽也沒有雨，天空嚴肅地灰著，大學對面的那座山好像才突然有份量起來。麗日高懸的日子我只感到它的快樂怡人，晨霧如紗的日子，我只感到它的空靈飄渺，但在這樣黯然的陰天，我才忽然發現它那種悲劇性的莊嚴。對著山，我第一次向這個城市傾出我的愛。

那時候，才想到這個城裡必然有許多憂憤的靈

不是遊記 | 不朽的失眠｜張曉風散文中英對照
Not a Travelogue | Immortal Sleeplessness

The scrolls of white paper placed by someone in the stairways of the building also became strikingly luminous in the night. In times of escape and flight, a high-rise building becomes some kind of dilapidated temple to shelter the homeless. The stairs can serve as beds, newspapers as coverlets, and even the wooden barrel of the Greek philosopher becomes a burden[10]. How naked can one strip life? How miserable is the misery of refugees in flight? The city stayed sleepless, so did I. In between sleep and wakefulness, only the colors rotated ceaselessly, playing the fading game of colors nonstop.

The Mountain

One day, there was no sunshine and no rain, just a solemnly grey sky. Only then did the mountain across from the campus obtain a prominence previously unseen. On sunny days when the sun shines high up in the sky, I can feel only the mountain's happiness; on foggy mornings, I feel only its elusiveness; it is only on a cloudy day like today that I feel the tragic majesty of the mountain. Facing the mountain, I pour out my love for this city for the first time.

It was then that I realized there must be many anxious and

10.——— *The author is referring to the Greek philosopher Diogenes, who allegedly slept in a wooden barrel at night, and basked in the sunshine by day. Once, Alexander the Great asked Diogenes if there was anything he could do for him. Diogenes replied. "Yes, don' t block my sunshine."*

魂，有許多淚，有許多澎湃的血脈。我不知道他們住在那一座木屋中？也許夜來時，他們同樣地飄流在彌敦道的人潮裡，我分不出他們的腳步。但我知道，在燈光之外，在層樓之外，在櫛比的櫥窗之外，必有一些有價值的靈魂，如同在海底的荒涼中，也有沉船中古美人的紅玉。

任濱海的比基尼戲水，任港外的舴艋舟衝浪，山只一昧地沉默。山在太平的景像之外，山在繁榮的畫面之外，山很傖然，山很傲然。

山的線條缺少柔和，山的顏色不夠明朗，在這嚴肅的陰天。山鬱鬱結結，如同深夜裡被抑壓在心底的哀歌。但山使我愛這個城，山使我想起那些陌生的靈魂，山使我想起那些不瞬的望鄉的眼睛。

不朽的失眠｜張曉風散文中英對照
Immortal Sleeplessness

angry souls in this city, a great deal of tears. I don't know which shacks they reside in. Maybe come nighttime, they wander among the crowds floating down Nathan Road. I cannot differentiate their footsteps from the stampede of the crowds. But I do know that, beyond the lights, outside the buildings, away from the shop windows, there must be some worthy souls, like the beautiful red jade that once belonged to some medieval beauty, buried in a sunken ship which now lies desolately at the bottom of the sea.

While bikini-clad women frolic by the beaches, and colorful sails ride the waves in the harbor, the mountain remains silent. The mountain, with its despondency and arrogance, stands aloof from the picture of halcyon days, keeping it's distance from the scene of prosperity.

On a grave cloudy like this, the contours of the mountain lack softness, and the colors lack brightness. The mountain is melancholic, like a sad song repressed to the depths of the heart in the still of night. But because of the mountain, I have fallen in love with this city, the mountain has reminded me of souls unbeknownst to me, and their unblinking homeward looking eyes.

吊頸嶺

所謂調景嶺，據說原來是叫做吊頸嶺的。

吊頸嶺很美，小小的屋子像白蕈一樣茂生在綠山坡上。山下是水，水也綠，綠得像舊式的絲綢。讓人怎麼也想不出二十年來的悲愁。

而吊頸嶺，那自盡者的故事，常躡足而來，在盛夏的窗下呢喃著流浪人的調子。

據說是許多年前了，一個猶太人買了這塊地，「這樣的山，這樣的水，」那猶太人想，「有一天會被珍視的。」

然而，沒有，那山那水和那片濃綠竟一直被拒絕。猶太人破產了，他茫然地站在自己的土地上，不相信地搖著頭。最後他以一根細繩結束了他自己——

Tiu Keng Ling

Some say the name Tiu Keng Ling[11] originally meant "Hang Neck Hill."

Tiu Keng Ling is very beautiful, with little houses decorating the green hills like mushrooms. Waters flow at the foot of the mountain, and the waters are green too, as green as ancient silk. The scene certainly does not evoke the sadness that spans two decades.

Yet Tiu Keng Ling remains haunted by the story of the suicide victim, who often tiptoes by, humming the nomad's tune beneath some window in the midst of summer.

It is said that many years ago, a Jewish businessman purchased the land on Tiu Keng Ling. "Given the mountain and the waters, the lot will increase in value some day."

However, it tuned out that the mountain, the waters, and the expanses of verdant green of Tiu Keng Ling continued to get neglected by land developers. The Jewish businessman went bankrupt. One day, as he stood on his piece of land, he shook his head in

---

11.——— Tiu Keng Ling: *better known as Rennie's Mill. Developed in the 1950s, it was built by refugees fleeing the Chinese Communist takeover in 1949. In 1905, a man named Rennie opened a noodle factory there. Having failed, he committed suicide by hanging himself (thus its Chinese name Tiu Keng Ling, a homophone for Hang Neck Hill). This place is called a "Taiwan loyalist area" by the people of Hong Kong.*

那失根的猶太人。

自懸是一個怎樣的動作啊！一種和泥土隔絕的死亡又是怎樣的死亡？

人行到山下，行到水湄，竟也能感到那種被扼的痛苦。相形之下，破產已不足為創傷，家破國裂之後還有什麼悲哀成其為悲哀？繩索也不成其為疼痛，背井離鄉之後還有什麼吊掛成其為吊掛？

那天中午，餐廳裡打起「生猛海鮮」的大字，心中便澀然地像被粗砂紙磨過一般。生猛，什麼海鮮還能生猛？在離水之後。低首看自己，和同行的，不曾踐踏過故土的小兒詩詩，二十年的淒楚便一下子翻湧而至。想起那天在一家水果店裡，正滿心怡悅地望著那些澳洲的、美洲的和台灣的漂亮水果，一旋身間卻在一個不惹眼的大竹簍裡發現「新鮮南京百合」的標籤。忽然，百合羹的記憶便那麼準確地來到舌尖，

disbelief, and hung himself on a rope—another wandering Jew.

What kind of an act is hanging oneself? What kind of a death is it that is suspended in mid-air, isolated from the solid ground?

I walked to the foot of the mountain by the sea, and actually felt the pain of being strangled. By comparison, bankruptcy is a much lesser pain than total estrangement from one's family and homeland. What greater suffering can there be? No rope can terminate the excruciating pain of being uprooted and stranded from home.

That day at noon, the living hall flaunted a sign with the words, "Seafood alive and kicking." My heart felt raw, as if it were abraded by coarse sandpaper. Fresh and bouncing? How can seafood, once out of the water, remain alive and bouncing? I look down at Shih-shih, who was with me, and who has never set foot on the motherland. Twenty years of anguish and bitterness engulfed me. I remember that day in a fruit shop. I was happily appreciating the beautiful fruit from Australia, America, and Taiwan, when, suddenly, I turned to find in an unassuming bamboo basket, a label which read "Fresh Nanking Lilies." All of a sudden, memories of

南京城的夏從看不見的角落拼湊而來。但最令人不能忍受的還是百合根上的那一團濕泥——像是用什麼人的眼淚和過的,那麼濕、那麼黏,那南京城的黑泥。我曾在其上躺過的,我曾以之做過手工的,南京城的泥。一剎間,我急急地轉身而去,覺得自己像一頭被追趕的獵物在千山間踉蹌。

有何海鮮能生猛?在離水之後。有何人能安然?在離土之後。吊頸嶺,使鄉魂黯然的又何止是這一嶺?使旅思沸滾的又何止是這一嶺。

吊頸嶺,遙遠的自盡者的幽泣在群峰間迴響,流落江左的異鄉人誰能沒有抹頸的劇痛。

——原載一九六九年十二月《現代文學》第39期

收入《愁鄉石》

the taste of lily stew[12] reappeared right on the tip of my tongue. Memories of Nanking summer flocked to my mind from unknown corners. What was most unbearable for me, however, was the soggy earth clinging on the lily root, the moist earth looking like it was mixed with someone's tears, wet and sticky. The black soil of Nanking. I had once slept on it, and molded it in my hands. At that moment, I hurriedly turned away, feeling like a staggering wild animal being pursued by hunters in the mountains.

Can any seafood stay alive and kicking out of water? Can any one, cut off from their homeland, stay alive and well? Tiu Keng Ling is not the only mountain where homesick souls turn even more forlorn. Nor is it the only mountain that causes a traveler's thoughts to simmer and boil.

The silent sobbing of the suicide victim echoes remotely in the peaks and valleys of Tiu Keng Ling. And no one, who has been uprooted and drifted to the left bank of the river, is exempt from the excruciating pain of a slash across the neck.

12.——— *Stew made of the bulb of lilies, which can be served hot or cold, considered to be a Chinese delicacy.*

畫　晴

Painting a Sunny Day

吳敏嘉／譯

Translated by Michelle M. Wu

其實即使有筆如雲，也不過隨寫隨抹，何嘗盡責描繪造物之奇。至於和風動草，大概本來也想低吟幾句雲的作品。只是雲彩總愛反覆地更改著，叫風聲無從傳布。如果有人學會雲的速記，把天上的文章流傳幾篇到人間，卻又該多麼好呢！

落了許久的雨，天忽然晴了。

心理上就覺得似乎撿回了一批失落的財寶，

天的藍寶石和山的綠翡翠在一夜之間又重現在晨窗中了。陽光傾注在山谷中，如同一盅淡薄的葡萄汁。

我起來，走下台階，獨自微笑著、歡喜著。四下一個人也沒有，我就覺得自己也沒有了。天地間只有一團喜悅、一腔溫柔、一片勃勃然的生氣。我走向田畦，就以為自己是一株恬然的菜花，我舉袂迎風，就覺得自己是一縷宛轉的氣流，我抬頭望天，卻又把自己誤為明燦的陽光。我的心從來沒有這樣寬廣過，恍忽中憶起一節經文：「上帝叫日頭照好人，也照歹人。」我第一次那樣深切地體會到造物的深心，於是忽然熱愛起一切有生命和無生命的東西來了，於是那樣渴切地想對每一個人說聲早安。

After days and days of rain, the sky suddenly cleared up. One felt as if lost treasures had been regained. Overnight, the sapphire blue of the sky and the emerald green of the mountains had reappeared in the morning window. Sunshine poured into the valley like a glass of sparkling grape juice.

I got up and walked down the stairs, smiling to myself and feeling happy. There was no one around, nor did I feel my own presence. Between heaven and earth, there was only a feeling of joy, a heart full of tenderness, and a pulsating sense of vitality. I walked towards the fields blissful remained and thought myself a serene flower. I lifted my arms up to the wind, and felt as if I were a gently swirling stream of air. I looked up into the sky, and mistakenly envisioned myself as the bright sunshine. My heart has never felt so open, and I drowsily recalled a passage from the Bible: "He causes his sun to rise on the evil and on the good..." For the first time, I experienced a heartfelt appreciation for the magnanimity of the Creator. Suddenly, I was deeply in love with everything animate and inanimate. I fervently looked forward to greeting everyone good morning.

　　不知怎的，忽然想起住在郊外的陳，就覺得非去拜訪她不可，人在這種日子裡真不該再有所安排和計畫的。在這種陽光中如果不帶有幾分醉意，凡事隨興而行，就顯得太不調和了。

　　轉了好幾班車，來到一條曲折黃泥路。天晴了，路剛曬乾，溫溫軟軟的，讓人感覺到大地的脈搏。一路走著，不覺到了，我站在竹籬面前，連吠門的小狗也沒有一隻。門上斜掛了一隻小鈴，我獨自搖了半天，猜想大概是沒人了。低頭細看，才發現一把極小的銅鎖——她也出去了。

　　我又站了許久，不知道自己該往那裡去。想要留個紙條，卻又說不出所以造訪的目的。其實我並不那麼渴望見她的，我只想消磨一個極好的太陽天，只想到鄉村裡去看看五穀六畜怎樣欣賞這個日子。

For no particular reason, I suddenly thought of Chen, who lives in the countryside, and felt an urge to visit her. One really shouldn't make any plans or arrangements on a day like this. Not to feel a bit tipsy, and not to act on one's whim in this kind of sunshine would be almost sinful.

Having transferred from one bus to another, I arrived at a winding yellow dirt road. It became was sunny, and the newly dried dirt on the road was so soft and warm under the sun that you could almost feel the pulse of mother earth. I walked along the road, and before I knew it, I was standing before a bamboo fence. There wasn't a single barking dog to greet me at the door. A little bell hung on the door. I rang it for quite some time and guessed that no one was home. Then I looked down to discover a tiny metal lock— she was out too.

I stood there for a long time, not knowing where I should go. I wanted to leave a note, but had no reason of visit to cite. Actually, I wasn't that anxious to see her. I just wanted to spend a perfect day in the sun, to see how the plants and animals in the countryside were enjoying this kind of day.

抬頭望去，遠處禾場很空闊，幾垛稻草疏疏落落地散布著，頗有些仿古製作的意味。我信步徐行，發現自己正走向一片廣場。黃綠不勻的草在我腳下伸展著，奇怪的大石在草叢中散置著。我選了一塊比較光滑的斜靠而坐，就覺得身下墊的，和身上蓋的都是灼熱的陽光。我陶醉了許久，定神環望，才發現這景致簡單得不可置信──一片草場，幾塊亂石。遠處惟有天草相黏，近處只有好風如水。沒有任何名花異草，沒有任何仕女雲集。但我為什麼這樣癡騃地坐著呢？我是被什麼吸引的呢？

我悠然地望著天，我的心就恍然回到往古的年代，那時候必然也是一個久雨後的晴天，一個村野之人，在耕作之餘，到禾場上去曬太陽。他的小狗在他的身旁打著滾，弄得一身是草。他酣然地躺著、傻傻地笑著，覺得沒有人經歷過這樣的幸福。於是，他興

Looking up, I saw an empty grain-threshing square in the distance, with only a few bundles of rice straw scattered about. The setting seemed somewhat like an imitation of a scene from antiquity. I strolled around, and found myself walking towards the square. Patches of yellow and green grass stretched under my feet, and curious looking rocks lay here and there. I selected a smoother one and reclined on it, feeling the scorching sunshine both cushioning me and covering me. I luxuriated in the sunshine for quite a while before collecting myself to look around, marveling at the incredible simplicity of this scene—a grassy meadow, and random rocks. In the distance, the grass joined with the sky. And close by, the gentle breeze was as refreshing as water. There were no exotic flowers and plants, nor were there elegant ladies in gathering. Then why did I sit so mesmerized? What was I attracted by?

I looked up at the sky dreamily, and my heart seemed to return to ancient times. It must have also been a sunny day after a long spell of rain. A man was basking in the sun in the grain-threshing square, having just worked in the fields. His little dog rolled by his side and became covered with straw. He lay there smiling, feeling like the happiest man alive. Then, getting all excited, he ran to the

奮起來，喘著氣去叩王室的門，要把這宗祕密公布出
來。他萬萬沒有想到所有聽見人都掩袖竊笑，從此把
他當作一個典故來打趣。

他有什麼錯呢？因為他發現的真理太簡單嗎？但
經過這樣多個世紀，他所體味的幸福仍然不是坐在暖
氣機邊的人所能了解的。如果我們肯早日離開陰深黑
暗的蟄居，回到熱熱亮亮的光中，那該多美呢！

頭頂上有一棵不知名的樹，葉子不多，卻都很青
翠，太陽的影像從樹葉的微隙中篩了下來。暖風過
處一滿地圓圓的日影都欣然起舞。唉，這樣溫柔的陽
光，對於庸碌的人而言，一生之中又能幾遇呢？

坐在這樣的樹下，又使我想起自己平日對人品的
觀察。我常常覺得自己的浮躁和淺薄就像「夏日之

royal palace, and knocked breathlessly on the king's door, wanting to announce the secret of his happiness. To his great surprise, however, everyone laughed at him in secret, making him the butt of their jokes.

What did he do wrong? Was the truth that he discovered too simple? Centuries have passed, and the happiness that he experienced then is still incomprehensible to people sitting in rooms with central heating. How wonderful it would be if we could leave the cavernous darkness of our chambers and step out into the warm and bright light!

Over my head was a tree that I couldn't name. It wasn't very lush, but every leaf was glistening green, with the rays of the sun filtering through the gaps of the leaves. When the warm breezes blew, the circles of sunshine on the ground all started to dance. Ah! How many times in their lives do those who live in quiet desperation get to enjoy the sunshine?

Sitting under the tree, I started to think about my observations of human behavior. I often feel that my restlessness and shallowness

日」，常使人厭惡、迴避。於是在深心之中，總不免暗暗地嚮往著一個境界——「冬日之日」。那是光明的，卻毫不刺眼；是暖熱的，卻不致灼人。什麼時候我才能那樣含蘊，那樣溫柔敦厚而又那樣深沉呢？「如果祢要我成為光，求祢叫我成為這樣的光。」我不禁用全心靈禱求「不是獨步中天，造成氣燄和光芒。而是透過灰冷的天空，用一腔熱忱去溫暖一切僵坐在陰濕中的人。」

漸近日午，光線更明朗了，一切景物的色調開始變得濃重。記得嘗讀過段成式的作品，獨愛其中一句：「坐對當窗木，看移三面陰。」想不到我也有緣領略這種靜趣。其實我所欣賞的，前人已經欣賞了；我所感受的，前人也已經感受了。但是，為什麼這些經歷依舊是這麼深、這麼新鮮呢？

身旁有一袋點心，是我順手買來，打算送給陳的，現在卻成了我的午餐，一個人，在無垠的草場

is like the "summer sun," unpleasant, and leading people to keep me at arm's length. Therefore, deep down inside, I aspire to reach a higher stage. I want to resemble the "winter sun." The winter sun is bright but not blinding, warm, but not scorching. When will I become as modest, gentle, honest, sincere and deep as the sun in the winter? "If you want me to become light, I beseech you to make me become such a light," I prayed wholeheartedly, "not to give off flame and shine high up in the center of the sky, but to penetrate through a steel grey sky and warm those who are sitting in the dark and dank."

Close to noon, the sun's rays brightened, and the color tone of everything became more intense. I remembered a line of verse by Duan Cheng-shih, "*I sit gazing at the tree outside the window, till it thrice shifts its shadow.*" Destiny has brought this serene joy into my path. What I have enjoyed has been enjoyed before me. What I have felt has also been felt before me. But why were these experiences still as profound and fresh as ever?

I brought with me a bag full of snacks, which I picked up on my way to Chen's and was meant as a present for Chen. It then became

上，咀嚼著簡單的乾糧，倒也是十分有趣。在這種景色裡，不覺其餓，卻也不覺其飽。吃東西只是一種情趣，一種藝術。

我原來是帶了一本詞集子的，卻一直沒打開，總覺得直接觀賞情景，比間接的觀賞要深刻得多。飯後有些倦了，才順手翻它幾頁。不覺沉然欲睡，手裡還拿著書，人已經恍然踏入另一個境界。

等到醒來，發現幾隻黑色瘦脛的羊，正慢慢地囓著草，遠遠的有一個孩子蹺腳躺著，悠然地嚼著一根長長的青草。我拋書而起，在草場上紆迴漫步。難得這麼靜的下午，我的腳步聲和羊群的囓草聲都清晰可聞。回頭再看看那曲臂為枕的孩子，不覺有點羨慕他那種「富貴於我如浮雲」的風度了。幾隻羊依舊低頭擇草，恍惚間只讓我覺得牠們嚼的不只是草，而是冬

my lunch. Alone, sitting in a field that seemed to stretch towards eternity, I munched on the simple food, which was a very interesting and unique experience. In that kind of setting, one does not feel hungry or full. The act of eating is elevated to a pleasure, an art.

I had a book of song lyrics with me, but never bothered to open it. Instead, I preferred to indulge myself in direct, first-hand experiences rather than vicarious observations. Only after the meal, feeling a bit tired, did I leaf through a few pages and, a numbing drowsiness coming over me, with the book clutched in my hand, and I dreamily drifted off to another world.

When I woke up, I found a few black goats slowly munching on grass, and a child lying on the grass in the distance, with one leg crossed over the other, chewing on a long stem of grass. I put down my book, sat up, and wandered up and down the grassy meadow. What a rare and quiet afternoon it was. I could hear my own footsteps and the munching sound of the goats. Eyeing the child lying on the grass with his arms cushioning his head, I started to envy his nonchalant and carefree attitude. The goats were still munching on the grass with lowered heads, and, in a daze, I felt that

天裡半發的綠意，以及草場上無邊無際的陽光。

日影稍稍西斜了，光輝卻仍舊不減，在一天之中，我往往偏愛這一刻。我知道有人歌頌朝雲，有人愛戀晚霞。至於耀眼的日升和幽邃的黑夜都慣受人們的鍾愛。唯有這樣平凡的下午，沒有一點彩色和光芒的時刻，常常會被人遺忘。但我卻不能自禁地喜愛並且瞻仰這份寧靜、恬淡和收斂。我回到自己的位置坐下，茫茫草原，就只交付我和那看羊的孩子嗎？叫我們如何消受得完呢？

偶抬頭，只見微雲掠空，斜斜地排著。像一首短詩，像一闋不規則的小令。看著看著，就忍不位發出許多奇想。記得元曲中有一段述說一個人不能寫信的理由：

> 不是無情思，遠青江，買不得天樣紙。

they were not just munching on the grass, but also the sprouting green in the winter, and the boundless sunshine in the meadow.

The sun's rays slanted a little towards the west, without losing any of its dazzle. This is the time of day that I love the most. I know that some people praise the dawn, and some love the pink and orange colors at dusk. Dazzling sunrises and dark velvety nights always appeal to people. But ordinary afternoons like this one, a time devoid of color and glow, are often forgotten and neglected. Yet I cannot help but love and adore the quiet, serenity and reserve of late afternoons. I returned to my place on the rock. Is this expanse of grass just for the goat-herding child and me?

On occasion, I lifted my head to watch the clouds float by in slanting rows. They resembled short poems, irregular short songs. As I gazed into the clouds, peculiar thoughts entered my head. I recalled a poem from the Yuan dynasty that explained a person's failure to write letters:

"It's not that I don't think of you, but having searched up and down the blue rivers, I could not find sky-like paper."

而現在，天空的藍箋已平鋪在我頭上，我卻又苦於沒有雲樣的筆。其實即使有筆如雲，也不過隨寫隨抹，何嘗盡責描繪造物之奇。至於和風動草，大概本來也想低吟幾句雲的作品。只是雲彩總愛反覆地更改，教風聲無從傳布。如果有人學會雲的速記，把天上的文章流傳幾篇到人間，卻又該多麼好呢！

正在癡想之間，發現不但雲朵的形狀變幻著，連它的顏色也奇異地轉換了。半天朱霞，粲然如焚，映得草地也有三分紅意了。不仔細分辨，就像莽原盡處燒著一片野火似的。牧羊的孩子不知何時已把他的羊聚攏了。村落裡炊煙裊升，他也就隱向一片暮靄中去了。

我站起身來，摸摸石頭還有一些餘溫，而空氣中卻沁進幾分涼意了。有一群孩子走過，每人抱著一懷

The blue letter paper of the sky was all smoothed out for me, but I lacked a pen that could write like the clouds. Even if I did have a pen like the clouds, I would only be able to scribble and doodle, never capable of describing the wonders of creation. The breezes caressing the grass may have chanted a few lines of verse written by the clouds. But the clouds were too capricious. Revising line after line, they made it impossible for the breezes to spread their work. How wonderful would it be if someone could learn the shorthand of the clouds and transcribe the writings in the sky for humanity!

Lost in reverie, I discovered that not only the shapes of the clouds kept changing, but the colors as well. Half of the sky was burning red, reflecting some of its glow onto the grass. Without careful scrutiny, one would wonder whether or not grassland at the far end were actually on fire. The goat-herder had already gathered his goats. Curls of smoke rose from the chimneys in the village, and the child's figure dissolved into the evening haze.

I stood up, touched and felt the lingering warmth of the rock, but there was already a slight chill in the air. A group of kids each carrying armfuls of sticks and straw passed by. They paused when

枯枝乾草。忽然見到我就都停下來，互相低語著。

「她有點奇怪，對不對？」

「我們這裡從來沒有人來遠足的。」

「我知道，」有一個較老成的孩子說：「他們有的人喜歡到這裡來畫圖的。」

「可是，我沒有看見她的紙和她的水彩呀！」

「她一定畫好了，藏起來了。」

　　得到滿意的結論以後，他們又作一行歸去了。遠處有疏疏密密的竹林，掩映一角紅牆，我望著他們各自走入他們的家，心中不禁憮然若失。想起城市的街道，想起兩側壁立的大廈，人行其間，抬頭只見一線天色，真彷彿置身於死蔭的幽谷了。而這裡，在這不

they saw me, whispering to each other:

"She's kind of weird, isn't she?"

"No one ever comes here on a field trip."

"I know," a more experienced kid said, "some people like to come here to paint."

"But I don't see her paper and her paints!"

"She must have painted her picture and tucked it away somewhere."

Having reached a satisfying conclusion, the children left. In the distance, a bamboo grove sheltered a corner of a red wall. I watched them enter their homes, feeling a strange sense of loss. I thought of the city streets, flanked by skyscrapers, with only a sliver of sky visible to those who craned their necks, resembling a valley of the shadow of death. Yet, sunshine flooded this nameless

知名的原野中，卻遍地氾濫著陽光。人生際遇不同，相去多麼遠啊！

我轉身離去，落日在我身後畫著紅豔的圓。而遠處昏黃的燈光也同時在我面前亮起。那種壯麗和寒愴成為極強烈的對照。

遙遙地看到陳的家，也已經有了燈光，想她必是倦遊歸來了，我遲疑了一下，沒有走過去搖鈴，我已拜望過郊外的晴朗，不必再看她了。

走到車站，總覺得手裡比來的時候多了一些東西，低頭看看，依然是那一本舊書。這使我忽然迷惑起來了，難道我真的攜有一張畫嗎？像那個孩子所說的：「畫好了，藏起來了！」

meadow, out in the countryside. Our destinies in life can be so drastically different!

I turned to leave, the setting sun a bright red circle behind me. Pale yellow lights in the distance also lit up before me. The magnificence and the bleakness formed a stark contrast.

Far away, I saw lights glittering from Chen's house. She must have returned home and was probably weary from her journey. I paused outside her house for a while, but decided against ringing her doorbell. I have already called on the sunshine in the countryside and I didn't have to see her anymore.

As I walked towards the bus station, I felt the weight of something in my hand. Looking down, I saw the same old book. But for a moment I grew confused. Had I really carried a picture away with me? As the child said, "She painted her picture and tucked it away!"

　　歸途上，當我們獨行在黑茫茫的暮色中，我就開始接觸那軸畫了。它是用淡墨染成的「晴郊圖」，畫在平整的心靈素宣上，在每一個陰黑的地方向我展示。

——選自《地毯的那一端》

On my way home, as I sauntered alone beneath the darkening sky, I started to feel connected to that painting. The picture, "Sunshine in the Countryside," painted in light ink on the rice paper of my heart, is now display for me in whatever dark place I find myself.

我不知道怎樣回答
I Don't Know How to Answer

吳敏嘉／譯

Translated by Michelle M. Wu

雖然我不知道怎樣回答他的問題，雖然我不知道用什麼方法使一個小男孩喜歡洗手，但有一件事我們彼此都知道，我仍然愛他，他也仍然愛我，我們之間仍然有無窮的信任和尊敬。

有些時候，我不知道怎樣回答那些問題，可是……

ॐ

有一次，經過一家木材店，忽然忍不住為之佇足了。秋陽照在那一片粗糙的木紋上，竟像炒栗子似的爆出一片乾燥郁烈的芬芳，我在那樣的香味裡回到了太古，我恍惚可以看到遮天蔽日的原始森林，我看到第一個人類以斧頭斲向擎天的綠意，一斧下去，木香爭先恐後地噴向整個森林，那人幾乎為之一震。原來，每一棵樹是一瓶久貯的香膏，一經啟封，就香得不可收拾。每一痕年輪是一篇古賦，耐得住最仔細的吟讀。

店員走過來，問我要買什麼木料，我不知道怎樣回答。我只能愚笨地搖搖頭。我要買什麼，我什麼都

Sometimes I don't know how to answer the questions, but...

∞

Once, passing by a lumber shop, my footsteps involuntarily ground to a halt. The autumn sunshine shone on the wood with there coarse grains, filling the air with a strong, dry aroma resembling fried chestnuts. Immersed in this aroma, I found myself back at the dawn of time, where I seemed to see primordial forests with dense foliage blocking the sun and the sky. I saw the first human being swing his axe into the green thicket that reached up to the sky. The first cut unleashed the woody aroma, which went off permeating the entire forest, sending a tremor of surprise down the man's spine. Every tree is a bottle of long preserved perfume, spilling its fragrance everywhere upon uncorking. Each annual ring is an ancient prose poem, inviting and withstanding the most detailed readings.

The salesperson walked over, asking me whether he could help me. I didn't know how to respond. I think I shook my head

不缺，我擁有一街晚秋的陽光，以及免費的沉實濃馥的木香。要快樂，所需要的東西是多麼出人意外的少啊！

8

七歲那年，在南京唸小學三年級，我一直記得我們的校長。二十五年之後我忽然知道她在台北一個五專做校長，便決定去看看她。

校警把我攔住，問我找誰，我回答了他，他又問我找她幹什麼？我忽然支吾而不知所答，我找她幹什麼？我怎樣使他了解我「不幹什麼」，我只是衝動地想看看二十五年前升旗臺上一個亮眼的回憶，我只想把二十五年來還沒忘記的校歌背給她聽，並且想問問她當年因為幼小而唱走了音的是什麼字——這些都算不算事情呢？

foolishly. What did I want to buy? I didn't want for anything. I had in my possession a street full of autumn sunshine, and the heavy, rich aroma of wood, all for free. How surprisingly little it really takes for one to be happy!

ॐ

When I was seven, I attended an elementary school in Nanjing, and I still remember the principal. Twenty-five years later, I found out that she was the principal of a junior college in Taipei. I decided to pay her a visit.

The school guard stopped me at the gate, inquiring whom I wanted to see. I told him, and he asked, "What is the purpose of your visit?" Suddenly, I found myself stuttering, at a loss for words—what did I want to see her for? How could I make the school guard understand that I had no "purpose"? I just impulsively wanted to meet that person who shines brightly in my memory from twenty-five years ago, the person who had stood on the platform during the flag-raising ceremony. I just wanted to recite to her our school anthem, and to ask her which word I had sung off-key because I was so small then. Can these reasons count as a purpose?

一個人找一個人必需要「有事」嗎？我忽然感到悲哀起來。那校警後來還是把我放了進去，我見到久違了四分之一世紀的一張臉，我更愛她——因為我自己也已經做了十年的老師，她也非常訝異而快樂，能在災劫之餘一同活著一同燃燒著，是一件可驚可嘆的事。

&

兒子七歲了，忽然出奇地想建樹他自己。有一天，我要他去洗手，他拒絕了。

「我為什麼要洗手？」

「洗手可以乾淨。」

「乾淨又怎麼樣？不乾淨又怎麼樣？」他抬起調皮的晶亮眼睛。

Must one have some "purpose" when one goes to see someone? I suddenly felt sad. The school guard eventually let me in, and I met the face that I had not seen for a quarter of a century. My love and admiration for the principal had grown—because I had been a teacher myself for ten years. She was also overcome by surprise and joy to see me. We had both survived war and catastrophe, and were both living and burning ourselves for the same worthy cause. This is an amazing and remarkable thing.

જી

My son is seven years old. Suddenly, he wants to make something of himself. One day, I told him to go wash his hands, but he refused.

"Why do I have to wash my hands?"

"Washing makes them clean."

"So what if my hand are clean? So what if they are dirty?" he answered, challenging me with his naughty and gleaming eyes.

「乾淨的小孩才有人喜歡。」

「有人喜歡又怎麼樣？沒有人喜歡又怎麼樣？」

「有人喜歡將來才能找個女朋友啊！」

「有女朋友又怎麼樣，沒有女朋友又怎麼樣？」

「有女朋友才能結婚啊！」

「結婚又怎麼樣？不結婚又怎麼樣？」

「結婚才能生小娃娃，媽媽才有孫子抱哪！」

「有孫子又怎麼樣？沒有孫子又怎麼樣？」

　　我知道他簡直為自己所發現的句子構造而著迷了，我知道那只是小兒戲語，但也不由得不感到一陣生命的悲涼，我對他說：

"Everyone likes a clean child."

"So what if I'm liked? So what if I'm not?"

"You have to be liked to have a girlfriend."

"So what if I have a girlfriend? So what if I don't?"

"You must have a girlfriend to get married!"

"So what if I get married? So what if I don't?"

"You have to get married to have a baby, so your mother can have a grandchild to hug."

"So what if you have grandchild, and so what if you don't?"

I knew that he was absolutely fascinated with his newly discovered sentence structure, and that they were just word games of a little boy. Nevertheless, a sense of melancholy swept over me. I replied,

「不怎麼樣！」

「不怎麼樣又怎麼樣？怎麼樣又怎麼樣？」

我在瞠目不知所對中感到一種敬意，他在成長，他在強烈地想要建樹起他自己的秩序和價值，我感到一種生命深處的震動。

雖然我不知道怎樣回答他的問題，雖然我不知道用什麼方法使一個小男孩喜歡洗手，但有一件事我們彼此都知道，我仍然愛他，他也仍然愛我，我們之間仍然有無窮的信任和尊敬。

——選自道聲版《曉風散文集》（1977年）

"Indeed, it doesn't matter at all."

"So what if it doesn't matter? So what if it matters?"

Not knowing how to respond, I felt a sense of awe mixed in my bewilderment—my little boy was growing up. He so very much wanted to establish his own world order and values. This realization sent a tremor to the core of my being.

Even though I didn't know how to answer his question. Even though I didn't know how to make a little boy enjoy washing his hands, there was something that we both knew: I loved him, and he loved me. Between us, there exists a never-ending bond of trust and respect.

給我一個解釋
Give Me an Explanation

吳敏嘉／譯

Translated by Michelle M. Wu

　　以後，每次走過別人牆頭冒出來的，花香如沸的樹蘭，微微的失悵裡我總想起那花匠悲冷的聲音。我想我總是肯同意別人的──只要給我一個好解釋。

|

後來，就再也沒有見過那麼美麗的石榴。

石榴裝在麻包裡，由鄉下親戚扛了來。

石榴在桌上滾落出來，渾圓豔紅，微微有些霜溜過的老澀，輕輕一碰就要爆裂。爆裂以後則恍如什麼大盜的私囊，裡面緊緊裹著密密實實的、閃爍生光的珠寶粒子。

那時我五歲，住南京，那石榴對我而言是故鄉徐州的顏色，一生一世不能忘記。

和石榴一樣難忘的是鄉親講的一個故事，那人口才似乎不好，但故事卻令人難忘：

「從前，有對兄弟，哥哥老是會說大話，說多了，也沒人肯信了。但他兄弟人好，老是替哥哥打圓

Part I.

I have never seen a more beautiful pomegranate since then. The pomegranate was in a gunnysack, brought by a relative from the countryside.

It rolled to on the tabletop, flaming red and very round, slightly weathered by the frost, looking as if ready to burst upon a light single touch. Upon bursting, it resembled the moneybag of a robber, tightly packed with glittering jewels.

I was five years old, living in Nanjing, and the pomegranate became the color of my hometown, Xuzhou, an impression seared into my memory for a lifetime.

Equally unforgettable is a story told by a relative. He did not seem to be a very good storyteller, but his story has stayed in my memory:

"Once upon a time, there were two brothers. The elder brother bragged a lot, to the extent that no one would believe in him

場。有一次，哥哥說，『你們大概從來沒有看過颳這麼大的風——把我家的井都颳到籬笆外頭去啦！』大家不信，弟弟說：『不錯，風真的很大，但不是把井颳到籬笆外頭去了，是把籬笆颳到井裡頭來了！』」

我偏著小頭，聽這離奇的兄弟，自己也不知道自己被什麼所感動。只覺心頭甸甸的，跟裝滿美麗石榴的麻包似的，竟怎麼也忘不了那故事裡活龍活現的兩兄弟。

四十年來家國，八千里地山河，那故事一直尾隨我，連同那美麗如神話如魔術的石榴，全是我童年時代好得介乎虛實之間的東西。

四十年後，我才知道，當年感動我的是什麼——是那弟弟娓娓的解釋，那言語間有委曲、有溫柔、有

anymore. But the younger brother was a kind person, who would always cover up for his brother. Once, the elder brother said, 'The winds were so strong that our well was blown outside the fence!' No one believed him, and the younger brother said, "It's true, the winds were very strong, only it's not that the well was blown outside the fence, but that the fence was blown into the well!"

I tilted my little head, listening to the story of these two odd brothers, not knowing what it was that touched me. My heart was weighted down, like the gunnysack full of beautiful pomegranates, and the story of the two brothers stayed imprinted in my mind.

The story has followed me all these years, along with the pomegranate. Which was beautiful as a myth and magic, these things from my childhood are so wonderful that they seem to be unreal.

Forty years on, I finally realize what it was that touched me—the younger brother's explanation, the benevolence, compassion and tenderness encapsulated in his words. Or, as the Confucians

慈憐和悲憫。或者，照儒者的說法，是有恕道。

　　長大以後，又聽到另一個故事，講的是幾個人在
聯句（或謂其中主角乃清代畫家金冬心），為了湊
韻腳，有人居然冒出一句：「飛來柳絮一片紅」的句
子。大家面面相覷，不知此人為何如此沒常識，天下
柳絮當然都是白的，但「白」不押韻，奈何？解圍的
才子出面了，他為那人在前面湊加了一句，「夕陽返
照桃花渡」，那柳絮便立刻紅得有道理了。我每想及
這樣的詩境，便不覺為其中的美感瞠目結舌。三月
天，桃花渡口紅霞烈山，一時天地皆朱，不知情的柳
絮一頭栽進去，當然也活該要跟萬物紅成一氣。這樣
動人的句子，叫人不禁要俯身自視，怕自己也正站在
夾岸桃花和落日夕照之間，怕自己的衣襟也不免沾上
一片酒紅。聖經上說：「愛心能遮過錯。」在我看
來，因愛而生的解釋才能把事情美滿化解。所謂化解
不是沒有是非，而是超越是非。就算有過錯也因那善

would say, the virtue of forgiving.

As I grew up, I heard another story, about a few people composing verse. One of the men, straining to rhyme, came up with the line, "Flying shreds of catkin blazing red." Everyone looked at each other, thinking, "The fellow is so ignorant, doesn't he know that catkin is white?" Of course, catkin is white, but white doesn't fit with the rhyme pattern. Right in the nick of time, someone came to the rescue by adding a preceding line, "The setting sun reflects on the peach blossom dock." Suddenly, there was an explanation why the catkin was blazing red. Whenever I think of the poetic scene, I am overwhelmed by its beauty. In March, the peach blossom dock is framed by mountains of red clouds which color the whole world red. The unknowing willow catkin stumbles into the scene, only to get dyed red as well. Such touching lines urge one to lean over to look at oneself, to see if one is standing between the shores lined by peach blossoms and the reflection of the sunset, to see if one's clothes are also saturated with burgundy. The Bible says, "Love covers all wrongs." In my point of view, explanations borne of love can settle all things. This does not mean that there is no judgment of right or wrong involved

意的解釋而成明礬入井，遂令濁物沉澱，水質復歸澄
瑩。

女兒天性渾厚，有一次，小學年紀的她對我說：
「你每次說五點回家，就會六點回來，說九點回
家，結果就會十點回來——我後來想通了，原來你說
的是出發的時間，路上一小時你忘了加進去。」

我聽了，不知該說什麼。我回家晚，並不是因為
忘了計算路上的時間，而是因為我生性貪溺，貪讀一
頁書、貪寫一段文字、貪一段山色……而小女孩說得
如此寬厚，簡直是鮑叔牙。二千多年前的鮑叔牙似乎
早已拿定主意，無論如何總要把管仲說成好人。兩人
合夥做生意，管仲多取利潤，鮑叔牙說：「他不是貪

in settlements. Instead, it implies that many things are beyond judgment. Even if someone has done wrong, let well-meaning explanations serve as alum in a well, causing impure particles to precipitate, and restoring the water to its purity.

My daughter was born good-hearted. Once, when she was in elementary school, she said to me, "Every time you say you would come home at five o'clock, you came back at six o'clock. When you say you would come home at nine o'clock, you ended up coming back at ten—I finally figured it out: what you meant is the time that you would depart for home, and you forgot to factor in the one hour of traffic time."

I did not know what to say in response. I returned late not because I forgot to factor in the traffic time, but because I am greedy by nature. I always want to read one more page, write one more paragraph, or linger a little longer in some beautiful surrounding...and yet my little girl makes such a generous assumption. Her generosity is almost comparable to Bao Shuya. Two thousand years ago, Bao Shuya made up his mind to describe Guan Zhong as a good man. In their joint venture, Guan Zhong

心——是因為他家窮。」管仲三次做官都給人辭了。鮑叔牙說：「不是他不長進，是他一時運氣不好。」管仲打三次仗，每次都敗亡逃走，鮑叔牙說：「不要罵他膽小鬼，他是因為家有老母。」鮑叔牙贏了，對於一個永遠有本事把你解釋成聖人的人，你只好自肅自策，把自己真的變成聖人。

物理學家可以說，給我一個支點，給我一根槓桿，我就可以把地球舉起來——而我說，給我一個解釋，我就可以再相信一次人世，我就可以再接納歷史，我就可以義無反顧擁抱這荒涼的城市。

2

「述而不作」，少年時代不明白孔子何以要作這種沒有才氣的選擇，我卻只希望作而不述。但歲月流轉，我終於明白，述，就是去悲憫、去認同、去解

took most of the profit, yet Bao Shuya said, "He is not greedy—it's because he's got a poor family to feed." Guan Zhong was dismissed from his official post three times. Bao Shuya said, "It's not that he doesn't work hard, it's just his bad luck." Guan Zhong fought in three wars, and fled in defeat every single time. Bao Shuya said, "Don't call him a coward, because his mother is old." Bao Shuya won. In face of someone who is so good at making you out to be a saint, you are left with no choice but to discipline yourself, and turn yourself into a real saint.

Physicists can say: give me a fulcrum, give me a lever, and I will lift the globe. But I say: give me an explanation, and I will believe in life once more, I will again accept history, and embrace this desolate city wholeheartedly.

Part II.

Confucius said, "I transmit the ancient and do not create." When I was young, I could not understand why he made such an unoriginal choice. I myself preferred creative writing to teaching. But as the years and months rolled by, I have come to understand

釋。有了好的解釋，宇宙為之端正，萬物由而含情。一部希臘神話用豐富的想像解釋了天地四時和風霜雨露。譬如說朝露，是某位希臘女神的清淚。月桂樹，則被解釋為阿波羅鍾情的女子。

農神的女兒成了地府之神的妻子，天神宙斯裁定她每年可以回娘家六個月。女兒歸寧，母親大悅，土地便春回。女兒一回夫家，立刻草木搖落眾芳歇，農神的恩寵也翻臉無情——季節就是這樣來的。

而莫考來是平原女神和宙斯的兒子，是風神，他出世第一天便跑到阿波羅的牧場去偷了兩條牛來吃（我們中國人叫「白雲蒼狗」，在希臘人卻成了「白雲肥牛」）——風神偷牛其實解釋了白雲經風一吹，

that to teach is to empathize, to acknowledge and to explain. Good explanations justify everything in the universe, filling all things with goodwill. Greek mythology has such richly imaginative explanations for the changing seasons and the wind, frost, rain and dew. For example, the dewdrops in the morning are the tears of a Greek goddess. The laurel tree is a transformation of Daphne, a nymph whom Apollo was infatuated with.

Demeter's daughter became the wife of Hades. Zeus decreed that she could return to her maiden home six months each year. When Persephone returns home, her mother rejoices, and spring rejuvenates the earth. When Persephone returns to Hades, the flowers wilt and the leaves fall off their branches. Demeter takes back her favors and turns a cold shoulder to the world—that explains the seasons of the year.

Mercury, the wind-footed messenger, is the son of Zeus and Maia. On the very day that he was born, he stole two cows from Apollo's farm. (The Chinese say "white clouds and black dogs" when describing the changing nature of things, the Greek equivalent would be "white clouds and fat cows.") Mercury stealing

便消失無蹤的神祕詭異。

神話至少有一半是拿來解釋宇宙大化和草木蟲魚的吧？如果人類不是那麼偏愛解釋，也許根本就不會產生神話。

而在中國，共工與顓頊爭帝，怒而觸不周之山，在一番「折天柱、絕地維」之後，（是回憶古代的一次大地震嗎？）發生了「天傾西北，地陷東南」的局面。天傾西北，所以星星多半滑到那裡去了，地陷東南，所以長江黃河便一路向東入海。

而埃及的砂磧上，至今屹立著人面獅身的巨像，中國早期的西王母則「其狀如人，豹尾、虎齒，穴處」。女媧也不免「人面蛇身」。這些傳說解釋起來

the cows explains the mystery of how white clouds dissolve into nothing in the wind.

At least half of all myths were intended to explain the how and why of the universe and the grass, trees, insects and fish. If human beings weren't suckers for explanations, there wouldn't be any mythology at all .

In China, the gods Gong-gong and Zhuan-xiang waged war against each other, and in his fury, Gong-gong gored the Bu-zhou Mountain, there by shaking the pillars of heaven and breaking the fibers of earth, (could this be a depiction of some earthquake in time immemorial?) causing the skies to slant toward the northwest, and land to sink towards the southeast. That explains why all the stars in the sky are found in the northwest, and why the Yangzi River and Yellow River flow all the way east into the sea.

The giant sphinx with the face of a man and body of a lion still stand in the midst of sand dunes of Egypt. According the ancient Chinese mythology, the Queen Mother of the West had the shape of a human being, the tail of a panther, the teeth of a tiger, with a

都透露出人類小小的悲傷，大約古人對自己的「頭部」是滿意的，至於這副軀體，他們卻多少感到自卑。於是最早的器官移植便完成了，他們把人頭下面換接了獅子、老虎或蛇鳥什麼的。說這些故事的人恐怕是第一批同時為人類的極限自悼，而又為人類的敏慧自豪的人吧？

　　而錢塘江的狂濤，據說只由於伍子胥那千年難平的憾恨。雅致的斑竹，全是妻子哭亡夫灑下的淚水……

　　解釋，這件事真令我入迷。

3

　　有一次，走在大英博物館裡看東西，而這大英博

cave for her home. Even Nuwa, the goddess in Chinese mythology who is responsible for the creation of mankind, has the head of a woman and the body of a snake. The way I see it, these legends reveal a little sad truth, that since ancient times, human beings have been satisfied with their heads but have had inferiority complexes when it came to their physiques. So these are the earliest organ transplants ever conducted, with the body of a lion, tiger, snake or bird taking the place of the human body. The storytellers of yore were probably the first to lament the limitations of mankind and yet take pride in human intelligence.

The roaring waves of the Qiantang River are said to represent the bitter regrets of Wu Zixu that will take more than a thousand years to overcome. And the spots on the spotted bamboo were the tears of a widow mourning the death of her husband...

Explanations have always fascinated me.

Part III.

Once, while looking around in the British Museum, I marveled

物館，由於是大英帝國全盛時期搜刮來的，幾乎無所不藏。書畫古玩固然多，連木乃伊也列成軍隊一般，供人檢閱。木乃伊還好，畢竟是密封的，不料走著走著，居然看到一具枯屍，赫然趴在玻璃櫃裡。淺色的頭髮，仍連著頭皮，頭皮綻處，露出白得無辜的頭骨。這人還有個奇異的外號叫「薑」，大概兼指他薑黃的膚色，和乾皺如薑塊的形貌吧！這人當時是採西亞一帶的砂葬，熱砂和大漠陽光把他封存了四千年，他便如此簡單明瞭的完成了不朽，不必借助事前的金縷玉衣，也不必事後塑起金身——這具屍體，他只是安靜的趴在那裡，便已不朽，真不可思議。

但對於這具屍體的「屈身葬」，身為漢人，卻不免有幾分想不通。對漢人來說，「兩腿一伸」就是死亡的代用語，死了，當然得直挺挺的躺著才對。及至回國，偶然翻閱一篇人類學的文章，內中提到屈身

at the sheer volume of items on display, all plundered when Great Britain ruled the world. There were books, paintings and artifacts galore, as well as an army of mummies for visitors to inspect. The mummies were okay, since most were kept in sealed coffins, but as I sauntered down the halls, I came across a withered corpse, crouching in a glass cabinet. The light-colored hair of the corpse still clung to the scalp, but a slit in the scalp revealed a patch of gleaming white skull. This person had a strange name, "Ginger," which probably is a reference to his ginger yellow skin, and parched ginger-like appearance! He was found buried in the desert region of West Asia where the hot sand and desert sun sealed and preserved him for four thousand years. He had somehow attained immortality in such a simple and straightforward way. With no need for jade outfits sewn with gold thread or gold encasements, his body, by just crouching there, had become immortal. This is truly incredible.

As a Han Chinese, I was baffled by the crouching position of the corpse. To the Chinese, "stretching out one's two legs" is a euphemism for dying. Death implies lying in a stretched out position with limbs straight and stiff. After returning home, I came across an anthropological paper that mentioned burial in the crawl

葬。那段解釋不知為何令人落淚，文章裡說：「有些民族所以採屈身葬，是因為他們認為死亡而埋入土裡，恰如嬰兒重歸母胎，胎兒既然在子宮中是屈身，人死入土亦當屈身。」我於是想起大英博物館中那不知名的西亞男子，我想起在蘭嶼雅美人的葬地裡一代代的死者，啊——原來他們都在回歸母體。我想起我自己，睡覺時也偏愛「睡如弓」的姿勢，冬夜裡，尤其喜歡蜷曲如一隻蝦米的安全感。多虧那篇文章的一番解釋，這以後我再看到屈身葬的民族，不會覺得他們「死得離奇」，反而覺得無限親切——只因他們比我們更像大地慈母的孩子。

4

神話退位以後，科學所做的事仍然還是不斷的解釋。何以有四季？他們說，因為地球的軸心跟太陽成二十三度半的傾斜，原來地球恰似一側媚的女子，

position. The explanation brought tears to my eyes. It said, "Some peoples adopt the crawl position in burial, because they think dying and returning to earth is comparable to a baby reentering the womb of its mother. Since babies are crouched up in the womb, so must the dead, when they return to the embrace of Mother Earth." This reminded me of the anonymous West Asian man in the British Museum, and generation after generation of Orchid Island's Yami tribesmen in their burial grounds...so, they have all returned to the womb of Mother Earth! I thought of myself, for I also like to curl up in sleep. Especially on winter nights, I like the sense of security that curling up like a shrimp brings. Thanks to the article, from then on, when I see people buried in the crawl position, I will no longer worry about their "strange and mysterious death," but feel a sense of infinite affinity instead—because they are more like the children of Mother Earth than us.

Part IV.

With mythology in retreat, science carried on with seeking and rendering explanations. Why are there four seasons? Because the Earth's axis forms a twenty-three degree angle to the Sun. So, Earth is actually a beauty that refuses to gaze directly at the Sun,

絕不肯直瞪著看太陽，她只用眼角餘光斜斜一掃，便享盡太陽的恩寵。何以有天際垂虹，只因為萬千雨珠一一折射了日頭的光彩，至於潮汐呢？那是月亮一次次致命的騷擾所引起的亢奮和委頓。還有甜沁的母乳為什麼那麼準確無誤的隨著嬰兒出世而開始分泌呢？（無論孩子多麼早產或晚產）那是落盤以後，自有訊號傳回，通知乳腺開始泌乳……科學其實只是一個執拗的孩子，對每一件事物好奇，並且不管死活的一路追問下去……每一項科學提出的答案，我都覺得應該洗手焚香，才能翻開閱讀，其間吉光片羽，在在都是天機乍洩。科學提供宇宙間一切天工的高度業務機密，這機密本不該讓我們凡夫俗子窺伺知曉，所以我每聆到一則生物的或生理的科學知識，總覺敬慎凜慄，心悅誠服。

詩人的角色，每每也負責作「歪打正著」式的解釋，「何處合成愁？」宋朝的吳文英作了成分分析以

but has somehow garnered all the Sun's favors simply by tossing him a glance from the corner of her eye. Why are there rainbows? There are rainbows because thousands and millions of raindrops refract the rays of the sun. What about the flow and ebb of the tides? They are climaxes and denouements caused by the Moon's fatal harassment. Why do mothers start lactating immediately following the birth of their babies? Regardless of whether the baby is born prematurely or overdue, when the placenta falls off, a message is sent to notify the mammary glands to start secreting milk...Science is actually an obstinate child, curious about everything, relentlessly pursuing questions to the end...Confronted with every answer presented by science, I feel that I should wash my hands and burn incense before leafing through the pages, because every single bit of information contained there in is a sudden revelation of some heavenly secret. Science provides us with the top secrets of the universe not meant for mortal eyes. I am held in awe and admiration whenever I come across excerpts of scientific knowledge on biology or physiology.

The poet's role just as often entails making explanations, lopsided as they sometimes may be. "Where does sorrow come

後，宣稱那是來自「離人心上秋」。東坡也提過「春色三分，二分塵土，一分流水」的解釋，說得簡直跟數學一樣精確。那無可奈何的落花，三分之二歸回了大地，三分之一逐水而去。元人小令為某個不愛寫信的男子的辯解也煞為有趣：「不是不相思，不是無才思，遶清江，買不得天樣紙。」這麼寥寥幾句，已足令人心醉，試想那人之所以尚未修書，只因覺得必須買到一張跟天一樣大的紙才夠寫他的無限情腸啊！

5

除了神話和詩，紅塵素居，諸事碌碌中，更不免需要一番解釋了，記得多年前，有次請人到家裡屋頂陽臺上種一棵樹蘭，並且事先說好了，不活包退費

from?" Wu Wen-ying from the Sung dynasty concluded after a componential analysis, that sorrow is the "autumn on a departing person's heart." （The Chinese character for sorrow is 愁；秋 stands for autumn, and 心 stands for heart）. Su Dong-po had his explanation contained in the line, "Three portions of spring, two portions of dust, and one portion of flowing water." This is almost as precise as a mathematic equation. Two-thirds of the helpless fallen flower return to dust, one-third get carried away by the flowing water. A Yuan poem's defense for a man who is not keen on writing letters is also very interesting: "It's not that I don't miss you, it's not that I don't want to write, but having crossed the clear rivers, I have not been able to buy sky-like paper." A few sparse lines, yet so very potent. To think that the reason why the person didn't write is because he felt he had to buy a piece of paper as expansive as the sky in order to do justice to his infinite longings!

Part V.

As in mythology and poetry, explanations play quite a large part in the hustle and bustle of day-to-day living. Years ago, I asked someone to plant a magnolia tree on my rooftop garden, and we

的。我付了錢，小小的樹蘭便栽在花圃正中間。一個禮拜以後，它卻死了。我對陽臺上一片芬芳的期待算是徹底破滅了。

我去找那花匠，他到現場驗了樹屍，我向他保證自己澆的水既不多也不少，絕對不敢造次。他對著夭折的樹苗偏著頭呆看了半天，語調悲傷的說：

「可是，太太，它是一棵樹呀！樹為什麼會死，理由多得很呢──譬如說，它原來是朝這方向種的，你把它拔起來，轉了一個方向再種，它就可能要死！這有什麼辦法呢？」

他的話不知觸動了我什麼，我竟放棄退費的約定，一言不發的讓他走了。

大約，忽然之間，他的解釋讓我同意，樹也是一種自主的生命，它可以同時擁有活下去以及不要活下

agreed that if the tree didn't live, I would get my money back. I made the payment, and the tree was planted in a pot. A week later, it died. My hope for a rooftop garden full of fragrant blossoms was totally dashed.

I sought out the gardener, and he examined the corpse of the tree on the spot. I explained that I had followed his instructions for watering the tree, no more, and no less. He tilted his head, gazed at the tree for a long time, and finally said in a mournful tone, "Madam, this is a tree! Why do trees die? There are many possible reasons—for example, if it were planted in this direction, and you pull it out, planting it in another direction, it might just die! There is simply nothing that can be done about it!"

His words stuck a chord somewhere in my heart, so I chose to overlook our previous agreement and let him go without a word.

Somehow, at that moment, I concurred with his explanation. A tree is also entitled to autonomy in life. It has the right to choose

去的權利。雖然也許只是調了一個方向，但它就是無法活下去，不是有的人也是如此嗎？我們可以到工廠裡去訂購一定容量的瓶子，一定尺碼的襯衫，生命，卻不能容你如此訂購的啊！

以後，每次走過別人牆頭冒出來的，花香如沸的樹蘭，微微的失悵裡我總想起那花匠悲冷的聲音。我想我總是肯同意別人的——只要給我一個好解釋。

孩子小的時候，做母親的糊裡糊塗地便已就任了「解釋者」的職位。記得小男孩初入幼稚園，穿著粉紅色的小圍兜來問我，為什麼他的圍兜是這種顏色。我說：「因為你們正像玫瑰花瓣一樣可愛呀！」「那中班為什麼就穿藍兜？」「藍色是天空的顏色，藍色又高又亮啊！」「白圍兜呢？大班穿白圍兜。」「白，就像天上的白雲，是很乾淨很純潔的意思。」他忽然開心的笑了，表情竟是驚喜，似乎沒料到小小圍兜

life over death or death over life. Maybe it was just an adjustment in direction that deprived it of its life force. Doesn't this principle apply to people as well? We can order bottles and shirts from factories, and have them made to specific shapes and sizes. In no way, however, can life be custom made!

Later, whenever I passed by gardens bursting to the seams with the fragrance of magnolia blossoms, I could not help but feel a little wistful, recalling the gardener's sad voice. I am always willing to concur with people—as long as I am provided with a good enough explanation.

When the children are yet small, mothers somehow take on the role of "explicator." I remember when my son was in kindergarten, he came to me wearing a pink bib. He asked me why his bib was pink. I said, "Because you are as cute as rose petals!" "But why do the bigger kids wear blue bibs?" "Because blue is the color of the big blue sky, bright and high!" "And the white bibs? The seniors wear white bibs." "White is the color of the clouds in the sky, clean and pure." He laughed, pleasantly surprised by my explanations. He had not expected a little bib to contain so many mysteries. I on my part was surprised by how little it took to make a little boy

裡居然藏著那麼多的神祕。我也嚇了一跳，原來孩子
要的只是那麼少，只要一番小小的道理，就算信口說
的，就夠他著迷好幾個月了。

十幾年過去了，午夜燈下，那小男孩用當年玩積
木的手在探索分子的結構。黑白小球結成奇異詭祕的
勾連，像一紮緊緊的玫瑰花束，又像一篇佈局繁複卻
條理井然無懈可擊的小說。

「這是正十二面烷。」他說，我驚訝這模擬的小
球竟如此勻稱優雅，黑球代表碳、白球代表氫，二者
的盈虛消長便也算物華天寶了。

「這是赫素烯。」

「這是……」

我滿心感激，上天何其厚我，那個曾要求我把整
個世界一一解釋給他聽的小男孩，現在居然用他化學

happy. My spur-of-the moment explanations were enough to keep him fascinated for months.

More than ten years have passed. The little boy sits under a lamp at midnight, exploring the structure of a molecule with hands that used to play with Lego blocks. The black and white balls converge into a strange and mysterious structure, resembling bundles of roses tightly bound together, or a novel with an impeccable structure binding complicated plots.

"This is dodecahedrane C2OH2O, " he said. I was surprised by the elegant proportions of this little ball, with the black representing carbon and the while representing hydrogen. The two meshed to heavenly perfection.

"This is isoprene."

"This is ..."

I am filled with gratitude. God has been very kind to me. The little boy who once begged me to explain the whole world to him

方面的專業知識向我解釋我所不了解的另一個世界。

如果有一天，我因生命衰竭而向上蒼祈求一兩年額外加簽的歲月，其目的無非是讓我回首再看一看這可驚可歎的山川和人世。能多看它們一眼，便能多用悲壯的，雖注定失敗卻仍不肯放棄的努力再解釋它們一次。並且也欣喜地看到人如何用智慧、用言詞、用弦管、用丹青、用靜穆、用愛，一一對這世界作其圓融的解釋。

是的，物理學家可以說，給我一個支點，給我一根槓桿，我就可以把地球舉起來——而我說，給我一個解釋，我就可以再相信一次人世，我就可以接納歷史，我就可以義無反顧的擁抱這荒涼的城市。

——原載一九九一年三月二十三日《中國時報》

收入九歌版《星星都已經到齊了》（2003年）

is now using his expert knowledge of chemistry to explain a whole new world to me.

If one day, I beg the Lord for a one or two year extension to my dwindling life, it will be because I want to look back on the magnificence of this world and this life. To cast one more glance at them, and to strive to make one more gallant though futile attempt to make sense of them. Also, to happily acknowledge how people attempt to explain the world around them with wisdom, words, strings and winds, colors, solemnity, and love.

Yes, physicists can say: give me a fulcrum, give me a lever, and I will lift the globe. I say, give me an explanation, and I will believe in life once more. I will accept history and embrace this desolate city wholeheartedly.

讀名家‧學英文01

不朽的失眠：
張曉風散文中英對照

作者	張曉風
譯者	彭鏡禧、吳敏嘉、康士林等
責任編輯	宋敏菁
發行人	蔡文甫
出版發行	九歌出版社有限公司
	臺北市105八德路3段12巷57弄40號
	電話／02-25776564‧傳真／02-25789205
	郵政劃撥／0112295-1
九歌文學網	www.chiuko.com.tw
印刷	晨捷印製股份有限公司
法律顧問	龍躍天律師‧蕭雄淋律師‧董安丹律師
初版	2011（民國100）年1月
定價	**320元**

書號	V0001
ISBN	978-957-444-726-8

（缺頁、破損或裝訂錯誤，請寄回本公司更換）

國家圖書館出版品預行編目資料

不朽的失眠：張曉風散文中英對照／張曉風著
; 彭鏡禧, 吳敏嘉, 康士林等譯.
-- 初版. -- 台北市：九歌，民100.01

面；　公分
中英對照
ISBN　978-957-444-726-8(平裝)

855　　　　　　　　　99017127